P9-DMP-073

MEGAN MEADE'S GUIDE TO THE McGOWAN BOYS

MEGAN MEADE'S GUIDE TO THE McGOWAN BOYS

a novel by **Kate Brian**

SIMON & SCHUSTER BOOKS FOR YOUNG READERS
New York   London   Toronto   Sydney

SIMON & SCHUSTER BOOKS FOR YOUNG READERS
An imprint of Simon & Schuster Children's Publishing Division
1230 Avenue of the Americas, New York, New York 10020

This book is a work of fiction. Any references to historical
events, real people, or real locales are used fictitiously. Other
names, characters, places, and incidents are products of the
author's imagination, and any resemblance to actual events or
locales or persons, living or dead, is entirely coincidental.

Copyright © 2005 by Alloy Entertainment
All rights reserved, including the right of reproduction in whole
or in part in any form.
SIMON & SCHUSTER BOOKS FOR YOUNG READERS is a trademark
of Simon & Schuster, Inc.

Produced by Alloy Entertainment
151 West 26th Street New York, NY 10001

Book design by Christopher Grassi
The text for this book is set in Horly Old Style.
Manufactured in the United States of America
2 4 6 8 10 9 7 5 3 1
CIP data for this book is available from the Library of Congress.
ISBN-13: 978-1-4169-0030-6
ISBN-10: 1-4169-0030-6

Prologue

"Megan, we need to talk."

Megan Meade swallowed a mouthful of root beer and let the bendy straw fall from her lips. Her heart dropped with it. She squeezed her eyes closed. What were her parents doing back from the base this early?

"This is my first soda of the day, I promise," she said, spinning in her father's leather swivel La-Z-Boy chair to face her parents. The moment she saw them, however, she knew they weren't about to talk about her daily sugar intake. This was much more serious.

Megan's parents stood before her in the living room of their cookie-cutter government-issue home, both wearing falsely excited smiles. They were also sporting their dress uniforms—her mom in an army green pressed skirt and jacket with dark panty hose, even though it was about a hundred and ten degrees in the Texas shade, and her dad with his collar buttoned so tight his neck was turning red.

"Oh God," Megan said.

She placed her sweating soda glass onto the coaster next to

her and braced herself. She'd been an army brat her entire life, so it wasn't hard for her to figure out what was coming next. She just hoped it wasn't true.

"It's time to pack your gear, Kicker," her father announced, forcing a boisterous grin. "We're moving to South Korea!"

Yup. There it was. Megan went into free fall. Her internal organs turned weightless and started floating around inside her body cavity. She clutched the arms on the chair so tightly her knuckles turned white, just to keep from throwing up.

"What?" Megan blurted. Her voice sounded very far away.

"It's been a while since we were transferred, hasn't it?" her father said matter-of-factly. "This should be exciting."

Exciting? Had he been testing gas masks over at the base today? How could anyone think she would be excited about this?

Megan had been moving all her life. She had been born in Rammstein, Germany, at one of the largest American army bases in Europe. When she was five, right about the time she had made her first friend, her family had been transferred to Turkey. After a few years there playing soccer with the boys and learning Turkish from her best friend, Medha, another transfer had come through, sending Megan to the country she had always thought of as home for the first time in her life. All through middle school Megan had moved, from Fort Carson in Colorado to Fort Bragg in North Carolina to Fort Leavenworth in Kansas. She hadn't been in any of those places long enough to make any real friends.

But here, at Fort Hood, Megan had finally found a home. She had made it through three full grades here. She was on a state-champion soccer team. She had just gotten her learner's permit.

She had a real best friend, Tracy Dale-Franklin. And this year, on the first day of school, she was going to talk to Ben Palmer. Finally, finally talk to him. She even had the outfit all picked out and had practiced her greeting three hundred and fifty-one times in front of the mirror. This was supposed to be The Year of Megan. Why was this happening?

"Megan? Aren't you going to say anything?" her mother asked.

Yeah, I'm gonna say something, Megan thought, standing up. She turned her back to her parents and stared out the window, hugging herself and gripping the sides of her T-shirt in her fists. This was so wrong. Megan had always been the perfect little daughter. She never talked back. She never let her parents know if she was depressed or upset or thought one of their many, *many* rules was unfair. She had never disobeyed them once in her life. And she was the only girl in school who wasn't strutting around the base in a miniskirt and belly shirt like the pop star du jour. Didn't her parents realize how good they had it?

As Megan glared out the window at the perfectly cut lawn, the impeccably kept flower beds, she felt like she always did right before she was going to throw up. And it was like an outside force was working on her; she knew there was no stopping what was about to happen.

She turned around and looked directly at her parents. She held her breath. "I'm not going."

It took every ounce of courage she had just to say those three words, and once they were out, she couldn't believe she had said them.

No one moved. Megan was having an out-of-body experience. Like last year when she had staggered over to the bench after suffering a concussion in the semifinal game at states. Like she was aware of what was going on around her but it wasn't really her that was there.

"Come again?" her father said.

"I'm not going. I'm not moving to South Korea," Megan said, still unable to believe the words had come out of her mouth.

Her mother and father exchanged a look. It seemed that they didn't think it was Megan in the room with them either.

"I'm sorry, Megan. We know this is hard for you," her mother said. "But we're only going to be there for two years and then you'll be back stateside for college anyway."

Two years. *Two years?* What kind of person put the word *only* in front of the words *two years?*

"No. I'm not going," Megan said, feeling braver every second her father didn't blow up at her. "You can't do this to me. This is my life and . . . and I want to live it *here!* With my friends! I mean, what about the soccer team? And . . . and the prom? And . . ."

Ben Palmer and his perfect dimples! her mind wailed.

"Megan—"

"I'm so sick of this, Mom! I hate moving. I just don't want to do it anymore. Why should I have to?"

Megan's father took a deep breath. His nostrils flared as he let it out. He and Megan's mother looked at each other again, silently communicating, as they so often did.

"Well, there is one other option," her mother said finally.

Megan barely dared to hope. "There is?"

"Your father and I—we have to go," Megan's mother said, fiddling with her wedding ring. "But if you really want to stay . . ."

"I can stay with Tracy?" Megan blurted.

"No . . . no," her father said. "The Dale-Franklins already have their hands full. You know that."

Megan knew all too well. Tracy's older brother, Joe, had graduated and was off at the Naval Academy, much to the chagrin of his "Go Army" dad. His moving out had freed up a bit of room in the Dale-Franklins' three-bedroom house, but Tracy still shared a room with her sister, Brianna, and the older of her two younger brothers was still bunking in the basement.

"Then what?"

"Well, last night Dad was speaking with John McGowan," her mother said.

"John McGowan?" Megan repeated, dumbstruck. John McGowan was her dad's old friend from med school.

"He said he and Regina would be happy to look after you while your dad and I are in South Korea," her mother continued, as if she hadn't just sent Megan's head spinning. "We didn't think it would be something you would be interested in. After all, South Korea is such an opportunity for a new cultural experience. However, if . . . you feel strongly . . ."

"John McGowan," Megan said again.

"Yes. John McGowan," her father said flatly. "Are you all right?"

Were her parents cracked? Were they certifiably insane? First they wanted to move her to the Far East, then they suggested shipping her off to the McGowan house in Boston, Massachusetts, to live with all those—

"The boys will take a little while to adjust, but I'm sure you'll all get along," her mother said.

Boys? Megan's mind was flooded with images of boys. Boys with missing teeth, their faces smeared with red Popsicle goo, their beady little eyes laughing at her as they lured her behind their house to see their new "puppy" and then lassoed her to a tree and hung her upside down. Greasy-haired, chubby-legged, evil little *boys*. Boys with worms in their pockets who ate gum off the ground and pulled her hair.

"How many of them were there again?" Megan asked as she lowered herself shakily onto the edge of the couch.

Her mother and father pondered this. "Seven at last count, I believe," her father said. "Quite a brood."

Yes. Quite, Megan thought.

Of course, they wouldn't be grubby-handed little mud-streaked munchkins anymore, would they? Most of them had been around her age the last time she saw them seven years ago, which meant that now they would be—gulp—*teenage* boys.

Megan started to sweat. Teenage boys were even worse. Mud-streaked munchkins she could clobber over the head with a wiffleball bat. That was how she had finally gotten pudgy, stringy-haired Evan—the worst of the pack—to back off the last time after the lassoing incident. But teenage boys—those she could not handle. Sixteen years old and she had yet to have a single functional conversation with a boy in her class. How was she supposed to live with seven of them?

"So, that's the deal," her father said. "You can either come to Korea with us or stay in the States, but if you stay here, you're staying with the McGowans."

"Do I have to decide right now?" Megan asked.

"No, sweetie, but soon," her mother said, leaning over to run her hand over Megan's strawberry blond hair. "We're leaving in a few days." She planted a kiss on Megan's forehead and Megan looked into her eyes—exactly the same green as Megan's own, with just a few wrinkles at the corners. "We'll miss you so much if you decide to stay."

Megan nodded numbly.

"But we just want what's best for you, so whatever you decide, we'll support you," her mother added.

Megan swallowed hard. This morning she had woken up with nothing more important to do than practice her Ben Palmer speech and add half a mile to her daily run. Now the whole world had turned upside down.

"Thanks," Megan said finally.

Her mother smiled, blinking back tears. "You think about it and let us know."

Megan slumped back into the couch as her parents left the room. *All by myself with seven boys or with my parents . . . in Korea,* Megan thought. Suddenly, running away to join the circus seemed like a workable option.

TooDamn-Funky: miss u already!!!

Kicker5525: Tracy! Im not even at the airport yet.

TooDamn-Funky: cant believe ur leaving me . . . L

Kicker5525: Not by choice.

TooDamn-Funky: u better email me the sec u get there! 7 boyz!! u r so lucky!

Kicker5525: Not lucky. Dead. Im dead.

TooDamn-Funky: well . . . tru. it IS u.

Kicker5525: Thx 4 the pep talk. Grrrr . . . HOW AM I GOING 2 DO THIS?????

TooDamn-Funky: hey maybe u will FINALLY learn 2 stand up 4 urself!!!

Kicker5525: How many times r u goin 2 say that 2 me?

TooDamn-Funky: 5,345,654. or til u start doing it.

Kicker5525: HEY! I stood up to MOM AND DAD!!!!

TooDamn-Funky: its a start. ok. been thinking bout the boyz. member last year my bro did that immersion thing in venezuela?

Kicker5525: where he learned to speak Spanish???

TooDamn-Funky: yeah! u go for 2 weeks & talk nothing but Spanish & u come back fluent.

Kicker5525: . . . ????

TooDamn-Funky: well this is like a guy immersion program!!!

Kicker5525: so . . . what. Im going 2 b fluent in GUY?

TooDamn-Funky: xactlee! u will c what they talk about when alone. U will c how they r with each other. U will c how they THINK!!! AND WHEN IT'S DONE YOU'LL BE ABLE TO WRITE A GUY GUIDE BOOK!!

Kicker5525: u r deranged.

TooDamn-Funky: IM SERIOUS! U culd break the guy code!

Kicker5525: Huh. Guy 101.

TooDamn-Funky: now ur getting it! and u WILL send me all ur notes so I can publish them on the web.

Kicker5525: i like it. im in. ☺

TooDamn-Funky: knew u wood b!

Kicker5525: Wish me luck!!! I sooooooo need it.

TooDamn-Funky: good luck! swak!

Kicker5525: swak back!

One

As Regina McGowan pulled her silver Volvo SUV into the driveway in front of the huge, farmhouse-style home, all Megan could see was boys. Boys everywhere. All seven of them plus their dad, running and laughing and shoving each other around on the front lawn, engaged in what appeared to be a full-contact, tackle version of ultimate Frisbee. They were playing shirts and skins. Shirts and mighty-fine-lookin' skins.

Megan's pulse pounded in her ears. Forget evil, laughing little monsters. These guys had been touched by the Abercrombie gods. They were a blur of toned, suntanned perfection. For a few seconds, Megan had trouble focusing on any one of them, but then one of the skins scored a goal and jumped up, arms thrust in the air, whooping in triumph as he clutched the Frisbee in one hand. His six-pack abs were dotted with sweat and a couple of stray pieces of torn grass. His smile sent shivers right through Megan's core. He had shaggy blond hair, a square chin, and the most perfect shoulder muscles Megan had ever seen. One of his brothers slapped him on the back and pointed toward the Volvo. He turned around and looked right at Megan.

The rest of the world ceased to exist.

"Well, here we are," Regina said, killing the engine. "Megan?"

He smiled slowly—a perfect, open, happy smile.

"Megan?"

Something touched Megan's arm.

"Oh! Uh . . . yeah?" Megan whipped her eyes away from Mr. Perfection and blushed.

Regina's brown eyes twinkled with amusement and sympathy. "You can live in the car if you want to, but they'll find a way to get to you anyway."

"Oh . . . uh . . ." *God, did she just catch me drooling all over one of her kids? Gross!*

"Don't worry. They promised me they would be on their best behavior," Regina said, unbuckling her seat belt. She swung her long dark hair over her shoulder as she got out of the car and leaned down to look at Megan. "My advice? Just be yourself. I'm sure you'll be fine."

Megan managed to smile and Regina slammed the car door. *Be myself. Yeah. Right. Because that's gotten me so far in the past.*

Megan's fingers shook as she reached for the door handle. She bit each of her lips in turn, wishing that she hadn't packed her one lip gloss in her suitcase, and tightened her ponytail as she stepped out of the car. Her light blue baby tee rode up a little bit whenever she moved and she was hyper-conscious of the fact that as she and Regina approached the group of boys, a few pairs of eyes went directly to her strip of tummy skin. Megan pulled down the hem of her T-shirt and crossed her arms over her chest.

"Megan! It's so good to see you!" John McGowan said, coming forward to greet her. He shook Megan's hand and stepped back to take a look at her. John was a tall man with blond hair that was longish on top but kept in place by some kind of crust-inducing product. He was wearing a Boston Red Sox T-shirt over sweat shorts and newish Nike sneakers. His skin was slightly weathered and wrinkled, but in a handsome movie star way rather than an aging dad kind of way.

"Yeah . . . you too," she replied.

"Well, you certainly have changed," John said. "The last time we saw you, you had that teddy bear permanently attached to your side, didn't you? What was his name again? Mr. Boo? Mr. Boony?"

Megan turned purple as the boys snickered. This was not happening. This *could* not be happening. Her *teddy bear*?

"John," Regina said in a warning tone.

"I don't really . . . remember," Megan lied. Everyone was staring at her.

"Oh yes, you do! You wouldn't put that thing down for the world!" John's voice boomed. "Mr. Binky? Mr.—"

"Mr. Boogie," she said.

The laughter was deafening.

"Yes! Mr. Boogie! I remember because you kept making him kiss me," John said gleefully. "You still have that thing?"

"Um . . . no," Megan lied. Mr. Boogie was tucked snugly at the bottom of her suitcase.

"Okay, I think that's enough of the trip down memory lane," Regina said, stepping up next to John and giving him a nudge.

"What? I'm just making her feel welcome," he said.

"Or exactly the opposite," Regina replied under her breath.

Megan stared at the ground, trying to ignore the nine pairs of eyes that were focused directly on her. The only time anyone ever really paid attention to Megan—other than her parents and Tracy—was when she was on the soccer field. And she was always blissfully ignorant of that audience because when she played, the rest of the world faded away. Now she felt more conspicuous than a full body rash.

"I think I'll just go get my stuff," she said, turning on her heel. With her back to the guys, Megan scrunched up her face, mortified. "Mr. Boogie? How does he remember Mr. Boogie?" She opened the rear door to the SUV and yanked out her backpack and her motorcycle helmet.

She slammed the door and whirled around, only to find herself face-to-chest with the Abercrombie god himself. Stunned, Megan tripped backward and slammed right into the side of the car.

Ow.

"Oops. Sorry," he said.

"It's problem," Megan said. *Oh God. "No problem" or "It's okay!" How hard is it to speak two words?*

"Sorry about my dad. We tried to trade him in, but there were no takers," he said with a slow smile. He had incredibly warm brown eyes.

Megan, of course, snorted a laugh. It was all she could do to keep from slapping her hand over her mouth and running away. This was already worse than any Ben Palmer encounter she had ever endured.

"Anyway, I thought I'd come help you with your bags."

"Uh . . . thanks," Megan said, sliding away from him and walking around to the trunk of the SUV.

"Nice bike," he said, glancing at the roof rack, where her silver-and-black Maverick was latched. Back at the airport Megan and Regina had ditched the dented cardboard box the airline had packed it in.

"Uh . . . thanks," she said again.

She slung her backpack over both shoulders, the helmet that was tied to it bouncing against her hip, and popped open the door.

"This is it?" he asked.

"Yeah," Megan replied.

"Wow. I thought girls were notorious for overpacking."

"I'm not much of a girl," Megan replied.

What? What did you just say?

He looked her up and down and smiled. "Could've fooled me."

If the human form could melt spontaneously, Megan would have turned to a puddle of liquid skin right then and there. This six-foot-four, gorgeous hunk of half-naked hottie was flirting with her! Inarticulate, tomboyish, freckle-nosed Megan Meade!

He hoisted the mesh bag of soccer balls out of the trunk and flung it over his shoulder. With his other hand he grabbed the large suitcase, leaving only her laptop bag and the smaller suitcase, filled with Megan's underwear, bras, and pj's, for her. Even though he had no idea what was in it, Megan was glad that she didn't have to watch him carry her lingerie up to the house.

"I'm Evan, by the way," he said as she reached up to slam the door.

Megan almost choked. "No."

Evan laughed. "Uh . . . yeah."

"You're Evan?"

Pudgy, stringy-haired, snot-bubble-blowing Evan had morphed into this WB-worthy god of Olympic proportions?

"Yeah, I am," he said, narrowing his eyes. "Didn't you hit me over the head with a baseball bat once?"

"It was a wiffleball bat," she said. "And I think you hung me from a tree first."

"Huh. I always thought it was a baseball bat," Evan said.

"I'm freakishly strong," she said.

Right. Stop talking now. Stop . . . talking . . . now!

But Evan was, in fact, still smiling. They started up the lawn toward the rest of the family.

"So, you're a soccer player, huh?" Evan said as they approached. "Good thing. You're gonna need to be quick to survive this crowd."

Megan looked at the other boys, who were now gathered in a huddle. The youngest one pushed between their legs to get into the middle of the circle, then pushed out again through another space and went in search of his next entry point.

"Yo! What's 'kicker' mean?" one of the boys asked, raising his head from the crowd. He had bleached blond hair cut in a Caesar style and a large diamond earring in his left ear.

Megan looked down at her motorcycle helmet as if she had never seen it before. Written across the back of the black helmet was the word *Kicker* in quotes.

"Oh, that's my nickname," Megan said.

"Lame nickname," Caesar Boy said.

"She plays soccer, idiot," Evan said as he placed her bag of soccer balls on the ground.

"Evan! Language!" Regina scolded.

"Okay, but tell him to quit being such a jerk," Evan replied.

Megan managed a smile.

"I can parent on my own, thank you," Regina shot back with a smirk. Then she walked over to Caesar Boy and gave him a light whack across the back of his head. He let out a dramatic "Ow!" and rubbed his skull vigorously, scowling.

"So, are you boys going to introduce yourselves, or are you all just going to stand there like a bunch of orangutans?" their father asked.

Grumbling, the boys broke up the circle a bit and one of them stepped forward. He was only slightly shorter than Evan, with a similar athletic build, wavy, tousled, dirty blond hair, and gray-blue eyes. He wore a black T-shirt that had one word on the front in white, old-fashioned typewriter lettering: *art*.

"Hey, I'm Finn," he said. His voice was on the soft side. He lifted his hand quickly in greeting. "I think you're gonna be in my class. Junior, right?"

"Yeah," Megan said.

"Cool," Finn replied with a smile. "Um, you met Evan," he said, then turned to the rest of the clan.

"This is Sean." He pointed to a shorter, stockier guy with dark brown hair and a bit of stubble. Sean wore jeans, even though it was ninety degrees out, and he had the Orange County Choppers logo tattooed on the outside of his right bicep. Megan and her dad had restored two vintage Harleys last year and she had just gotten her motorcycle permit. Sean might be a kindred spirit under that blank expression.

"That's Doug," Finn said, pointing out Caesar Boy, who clearly thought he was the second coming of Eminem. He wore a gold cross around his neck and had big, defined arms but an incongruously pudgy stomach. Megan smiled at him, but he looked away from her and sucked his teeth.

"This is Miller," Finn said. Miller had a blond crew cut and was sporting a New York Yankees T-shirt with a caricature of A-Rod on the front. He stared at the ground and only nodded slightly when Finn said his name.

"That's Ian," Finn said, pointing at a chubby kid who looked much like Megan remembered Evan looking seven years ago.

"Hi, Ian," Megan said.

"Hi, *Kicker*," Ian replied, cackling a laugh and holding his stomach.

Wow. He is exactly *like Evan was seven years ago,* Megan thought.

Out of nowhere the littlest one came running over, making a random revving noise. He ran headfirst into Evan's knees and laughed.

"And this runt is Caleb," Evan said, lifting the little boy like he was hoisting a bag of potatoes. Caleb sat comfortably in the crook of Evan's arm with his head against Evan's chest and one arm around his back. He touched the tip of his finger to his mouth, smiled shyly, and said, "Hi, Megan."

Megan took a deep breath. "Hi, Caleb."

Three for seven, she thought. *Could be worse.*

From: Kicker5525@yahoo.com
To: Tom-n-JeanMeade@yahoo.com
Subject: Settling in
Hey Mom and Dad!

Just wanted to let you know everything is fine here. We had barbecue for dinner and I ate a salad with it, I promise. The boys are getting used to me and Regina and John are really nice. Can't wait to see the new school tomorrow. I miss you guys already. Hope you had a good flight! E-mail and call me as soon as you can.

Love,

Megan

Megan sat back in the window seat of her new bedroom with her laptop propped up in front of her knees. There was one thing Megan could say for her new digs—they were definitely pink. The walls were pink, the bedspread was pink, the flower-shaped throw rug on the wood floor was pink. Regina had even decorated the white dresser with large pink flower decals.

It was the exact opposite of every room Megan had ever lived in.

There was a quick knock on the door and Regina stuck her head in. Megan sat up a little straighter.

"I brought you some towels for the morning," Regina said with a smile, placing pink towels on the end of the bed. She looked around the room and paused when she saw the still-packed suitcases. "Settling in okay?"

"Yes, ma'am. Thank you," Megan said automatically. She would get around to unpacking eventually, but that would make things seem so final. She needed to get used to the fact that this was actually her space first. She needed to get used to the pink.

"You don't have to call me ma'am," Regina said, crossing her arms over her chest and shrugging. "Makes me feel old."

"Oh. Okay, ma—" Megan bit her tongue. This was definitely going to take getting used to.

"So, I was thinking we could go shopping tomorrow night," Regina suggested. "I'm sure there are some things you still need to get for school. New clothes . . . makeup . . . maybe a new purse?"

Wow. This woman is hurting for female companionship, Megan thought.

"Uh . . . okay. Sure," she said, even though she had everything she needed. Megan didn't exactly enjoy shopping—a quality that had always puzzled queen-of-the-bargain-hunt Tracy—but she knew she could make the sacrifice when her answer was rewarded with an even huger smile from Regina.

"Great! I know just where to take you. There's a whole new wing on the mall that I've been dying to check out," Regina said. "We'll eat at the food court and have a real girls' night."

"Sounds great," Megan said. *New wing on the mall? Food court?*

"Okay, well, good night," Regina said. "Let me know if you need anything."

"Regina?" Megan said, stopping her as she backed out of the room. "Is it always this . . . quiet around here?"

Regina's brows furrowed. "Basically never. I think we have you to thank for our current peace and quiet. My boys aren't quite sure how to behave with an actual girl around."

Just what I didn't want to hear, Megan thought, a lump forming in her throat. After a quiet dinner during which John and Regina had made all the conversation, the boys had retreated to the basement and their Xbox and Megan hadn't heard from any of them since. It felt distinctly like a freeze-out. While she didn't mind avoiding their scrutiny, she didn't want the boys to hate her, either.

"I hope I'm not making anyone . . . uncomfortable."

"Please," Regina said with a wave of her hand. "I may actually get my first good night's sleep in twenty years. Good night, Megan."

"'Night," Megan said.

As the door closed, Megan sighed and reread her message to her parents. *"The boys are getting used to me."* Part of her felt guilty for not telling them the whole truth—that the boys were ignoring her and were clearly put out by her presence—but what was the point? She placed her finger on the mouse and clicked send.

Somewhere in the house a floorboard creaked and an outer door slammed; then all was quiet again. This place was definitely not the nuthouse she had expected.

The next morning Megan opened her door slowly and peeked out into the hallway. Music played from behind one of the closed doors, but the hall was empty and the bathroom door across the way was open. Now was her chance.

Clutching her shower things to her chest, she stepped out at the exact same moment Finn emerged from his room. Megan stopped in her tracks. His wavy hair stuck up in the back and he was wearing a pair of faded Boston College mesh shorts and a white T-shirt. So this was what boys slept in.

"Oh . . . hey. You going in there?" Finn asked.

"Yeah, if it's okay," Megan said. "I mean, I don't have to right now. I don't want to mess up your morning routine."

"No, go ahead," Finn said. "Knock on my door when you're done?"

"Sure. Okay," Megan said. "No problem."

After a quick shower in which she tried not to dwell on the dozens of tiny dark and blond hairs stuck to every surface, Megan wrapped her hair up in a towel and slipped back into her pajamas. It sounded like there was a little more activity in the hallway now. She took a deep breath and wondered if it was always going to be this intimidating to simply move around the house.

Squaring her shoulders, Megan stepped out into the hall and her bare foot was almost flattened by a remote-control car. She jumped out of the way just in time and watched the thing zip down the hall and hop a makeshift ramp. Megan's eyes widened in horror as she saw what was at the other end of the jump.

Oh . . . my . . . God!

The car slammed into a mountain of wrapped tampons, which exploded all over the hallway at impact. Ian raced past her, laughing maniacally, wielding the controls. Doug came out of his room to check out the commotion, picked up one of the tampons, and smirked.

"Super-absorbency?" he said, just as Evan and Finn emerged from their rooms on opposite sides of the hall.

"What's super-absorbency?" Ian asked, his forehead wrinkling.

"I don't even want to know," Doug replied, chucking the tampon in Megan's direction. She caught it, feeling like her body temperature could singe a hole in the rug. Doug laughed and took off down the stairs with Ian barreling after him.

"Ignore him. We all do," Evan said with a groggy smile.

"Uh . . . dude," Finn said, glancing down at Evan's boxers, which were covered in cartoon frogs and gaping open. Then Finn glanced over at Megan.

Then Evan went back into his room and closed the door. No shame whatsoever.

"Here, I'll . . . help you clean this up," Finn said, dropping to the floor and picking up a few tampons.

"No!" Megan lurched forward and Finn fell back from his knees to his butt. She grabbed the tampons from his hands. "I'd really rather you didn't."

"But I can—"

"No. Just . . . I'm fine," Megan said, awkwardly gathering up the slippery wrappers in her arms. "Thanks."

"Okay," Finn said.

He stood and hovered for a second, prolonging Megan's mortification. Finally Finn walked into the bathroom and shut the door. Left alone, it was all Megan could do to keep from bursting into tears. They had been in her room. They had gone through her stuff. And Evan had seen her *tampons*.

This was definitely the worst morning of her life.

Megan stood up, clamped her things to her chest, walked into her room, and dropped everything on her bed.

Okay, get a grip, she told herself. *It could have been worse. Somehow.*

With a deep, bolstering breath, she started to lift her pajama top over her head but then saw something out of the corner of her eye and screamed. Doug and Ian were now in the oak tree in the backyard, armed with binoculars, looking right through her window.

"What are you *doing?*" Megan shouted.

Doug snickered and waved. "How ya like my room?"

"*Your* room?"

"Hey, I don't mind bunking with Mill the Dill Hole if I get to check out his view," Doug called with a laugh.

Jaw hanging open, Megan yanked on the cord next to the window, lowering the blinds.

"Kids! Breakfast!" Regina shouted from downstairs. "If you don't get your butts down here in the next five minutes, you're all going to be late!"

Deep breath, Megan told herself. She grabbed the wooden chair from in front of her desk and jabbed it under the doorknob as she had seen done so many times in the movies. Dropping to her knees, she opened her large suitcase and her shoulders slumped.

"What the?"

There were purple marks all over the front of her favorite white T-shirt. She picked it up and unfolded it. Drawn right on the front were two huge circles, each with a dot in its center. Breasts. From their simple rendering it was clear they had been drawn by one of the younger boys. And it wasn't just this shirt. Someone had drawn on three of her favorite tees. Did John and Regina know that their kids were criminally insane?

Just breathe, Megan told herself. She tossed the T-shirts in the garbage can by the desk. She took out her heather gray army tee and got dressed quickly, then blew her hair half dry and put it back in a ponytail. Suddenly she couldn't wait to get to school. It had to be a hell of a lot better than this place. How had she ever thought that last night's peace and quiet was disturbing?

She opened the closet door to grab her sneakers and tripped back in surprise. Caleb was standing right in front of her with her pink bra tied around his head, the cups sticking up like ears.

"Ha ha ha! Scared ya!" Caleb's little tongue wagged as he laughed.

Megan's heart was pounding. She made a grab for him, but he shot right past her.

"I got your bra-ah! I got your bra-ah!" he sang, dancing around in her room.

"Caleb!" Megan shouted, lunging.

The little sucker was too quick. He dodged her fingers, yanked the chair down with a crash, and made a break for it. Megan chased him to the stairs, but Caleb straddled the banister and slid down it, his feet hitting the ground before Megan could even make it to the second step. He turned, grinned at her, and headed for the kitchen.

"Caleb! No!" Megan wailed.

Down in the kitchen the rest of the boys were talking and laughing and chowing down. Megan barreled down the staircase and raced through the living room.

Megan rounded the corner into the hallway just as Caleb was about to push through the swinging door.

"Stop!" she shouted.

Just then Sean appeared out of nowhere. He grabbed the little guy around the waist with one arm and hauled him up.

"Lemme go! Lemme go!" Caleb shouted over and over again.

Sean snapped the bra from Caleb's head and handed it to Megan. Megan just stood where she was. She had no idea what to say or do.

"There's no controlling that one," Sean said. They were the first words Megan had heard him speak.

"Yeah . . . thank you," Megan replied. "If he had gotten in there . . ."

Sean looked at her for a moment. His brown hair stood straight up and there was a streak of blackish-green grease below his right ear. He was handsome in a rugged, dangerous kind of way, but there was something about him that was off-putting. Maybe it was the appraising and almost quizzical way that he was staring at her. Like he wasn't quite sure what she was.

"Yeah, well," he said.

Then he turned and walked back down a short hallway. Megan watched as he opened the door that led to the garage. The acrid smell of cigarette smoke hit her nostrils and she caught a glimpse of a couple of guys and a girl lounging on an old set of living room furniture. Everyone was wearing black. There was a drum set in the center of the garage, surrounded by amps and microphones. Just before the door closed again, Megan saw the back end of a mint Harley, its side panels gleaming as if it had been recently waxed.

Megan leaned back and took a deep breath. Apparently Sean was in a band. And the motorcycle had to be his. Maybe one day she would ask him about it. If a day ever came when she felt comfortable under that gaze of his.

For now, finding a hiding place for her bras, panties, and tampons was a far more important priority. Megan ignored her grumbling stomach, turned away from the kitchen, and trudged back upstairs.

From: Kicker5525@yahoo.com
To: TooDamn-Funky@rockin.com
Subject: Boy Guide

Megan Meade's Guide to the McGowan Boys
Entry One

Observation #1: When they're beautiful, they know they're beautiful.

Like the second-to-oldest one, Evan. He's a senior. He is perfection personified. And he knows it. You can tell because he just sort of smiles knowingly when you gape at him. Not that I've been gaping at him. Not at all. Anyway, too soon yet to tell if it negatively affects his behavior. (Like Mike Blukowsi and his Astrodome-sized ego problem.)

Observation #2: They like skin.

Especially skin they think they're not necessarily supposed to be seeing. Like the space between your belly tee and your waistband.

Observation #3: They have no problem bringing up events that would mortify me into shamed silence if the roles were reversed.

Like Evan totally brought up the wiffleball bat incident, when if that had happened to me, I'd be wishing on every one of my birthday cakes for everyone to forget it.

Observation #4: They gossip.

Can you believe it? I overheard Finn and Doug in the backyard talking about some girl named Dawn who blew off some guy named Simon for some other guy named Rick for like TWENTY MINUTES! They sounded like those old mole-hair ladies at Sal's Milkshakes. 'Member the ones who lectured us for a whole hour that day about how young women shouldn't wear shorts? Wait, okay, I got sidetracked.

Observation #5: The older ones are so cute with the younger ones.

They were playing ultimate Frisbee when I first got here and Evan totally let Caleb and Ian tackle him. It was soooooo cute. **sigh**

Observation #6: They're cliquey.

I mean, eye-rolling, secret-handshake, don't-talk-to-us-unless-you've-got-an-X-and-a-Y cliquey. Very schooled in the art of the freeze-out.

Observation #7: They have no sense of personal space.

I need a lock on my door. STAT.

Observation #8: Boys are icky.

Do not even get me started on the state of the bathroom. I'm thinking of calling in a haz-mat team. Seriously.

Observation #9: They have really freaky things going on down there.
Yeah, I don't think I'm ready to elaborate on that one yet.

Observation #10: They know how to make enemies.
Big time.

Two

"Yo, dorkus! Pass the Cocoa Puffs!"

"What the? Who drank all the orange juice?"

"Coffee's ready! Who wants?"

Megan walked into the kitchen, noted the mayhem at the breakfast table, and joined Regina at the center island, where the coffee was brewing.

"Good morning, Megan!" Regina said brightly. She glanced at Megan's outfit—army tee and frayed boy jeans—and her smile became slightly strained. "You look . . . comfortable."

"I am," Megan replied. "Mind if I have some?" She gestured at the coffee.

"Please! Feel free," Regina replied. "This is your house now."

Actually, I think this house belongs to the crazies at the table, Megan thought, reaching for the pot. She couldn't believe that after everything the younger McGowans had done to her that morning, they were all just crunching away at their cereal, totally guilt-free. They didn't even seem worried that she would tell. Maybe they could just tell that Megan wasn't the tattling type.

"Listen, Regina . . . did I really take Doug's room?" Megan asked, lowering her voice.

"Why? Is he torturing you about it?" Regina asked.

"No, it's just . . . I don't want to put anybody out."

"Please don't give it another thought," Regina said, touching Megan's hand. She leaned in closer and whispered, "Between you and me, Doug *needed* to be knocked down a peg."

Megan smiled awkwardly and filled her mug with coffee. Miller walked in and stood next to his mother. He held one arm straight down at his side and gripped his elbow with his other hand so that his arms formed a number four across his body. He looked down at the floor.

What was his deal? Miller had yet to make eye contact with Megan since she had arrived. Megan knew what it was like to be awkward around strangers, but this was taking it to a whole new level.

"Hey, Miller," Megan tried.

He didn't answer. Trying not to feel slighted, Megan spooned some sugar into her mug from the sugar bowl. She was just going to have to accept the fact that this was not her morning. She added a little half-and-half to her coffee and stirred.

"That doesn't go there."

Megan looked up. Miller was staring at the half-and-half carton intently and gripping his arm even more tightly than before. Regina had her back to them now as she dug through the refrigerator.

"What?" Megan asked, her heart thumping.

"That doesn't go there," he said again. For a split second his eyes actually rested on Megan. It was the first time she had seen them. They were a clear, sharp blue. "That doesn't go there," he repeated. "It doesn't go there."

Megan's pulse started to race. "I'm sorry. . . . What doesn't go where?"

"That doesn't go there," Miller said again, a severe flush rising from his neck up to his temples. His voice was growing more and more intense.

Megan backed up a step. "I'm sorry. I don't—"

"Miller likes to keep all the bottles and cartons in height order," Regina said, placing her hands on Miller's shoulders. Her touch seemed to calm him a little.

"That doesn't go there," he said in a more explanatory tone.

"Oh . . . okay," Megan said.

She felt like every vein in her body was throbbing as Miller watched her intently. The items on the island were, in fact, lined up in height order, from the coffeemaker down to the pitcher of milk, the coffee canister, and the sugar bowl. Megan picked up the half-and-half carton, her hand shaking slightly, and placed it back in the space it had been in before, right between the coffee canister and the sugar.

Miller smiled, satisfied.

"Miller, this is Megan," Regina said, leaning over his shoulder. "You remember we talked about Megan coming to live here, right? Did you say hello yet?"

"Hello," Miller said to the floor.

"Hi," Megan replied.

"Did you know Joe DiMaggio holds the Major League Baseball record for the longest consecutive game hitting streak at fifty-six games?" he asked, glancing up briefly. "He set it in 1941 as a member of the New York Yankees."

Megan looked at Regina again, who nodded in an encouraging way. "Really?" she said. "I'll have to remember that."

Miller nodded and looked at his mother before focusing on the floor again and walking off toward the breakfast table. Megan suddenly had no idea where to look. What was that all about? And why did she feel so frightened?

"Your parents didn't tell you about Miller, huh?" Regina asked in a hushed voice.

Megan swallowed hard and placed her coffee on the counter. "What about him?"

"He has Asperger's syndrome. It's a form of autism," Regina said. "Do you know anything about it?"

"Not really," Megan said, turning to watch Miller as he talked with Finn. "I mean, I've heard of autism, but . . ."

"It takes all kinds of forms, but basically it's a social dysfunction," Regina said, stepping up next to Megan. "With Miller, it's a few things. First, he has to have things arranged just so or he gets agitated, which you just saw. Second, he's not great with new people, but clearly he likes you."

"He does?" Megan asked.

"Usually he doesn't talk to a new person for at least a week. With you it only took overnight," Regina said. "Third, he's incredible at math and memorization and he has a knack for stats. His particular obsession is—"

"The New York Yankees," Megan finished, glancing at the Derek Jeter jersey he was sporting.

"Exactly," Regina said with a nod. "You can imagine how my die-hard Red Sox fan husband feels about one of his sons worshiping the Evil Empire." Regina chuckled. "Anyway, if you have any questions about Asperger's or anything, Megan, just let us know. Miller is a great kid. He just needs a little bit of extra attention, that's all."

"Got it," Megan said.

As Regina went about straightening the kitchen, Megan stood off to the side of the action, sipping her coffee. At the far end of the table, Caleb sneezed and Megan watched, surprised, as Doug lifted a napkin to the kid's nose and helped him blow. Then he ruffled Caleb's hair and got up to dump the napkin in the trash.

Okay, so maybe he isn't the devil, Megan thought. Of course, this didn't change the fact that her blinds were never coming up again.

Doug grabbed a mug from the counter and poured himself some coffee. Megan noticed that the leg of his jeans was heavily decorated. The entire thigh was covered in an intricate doodle of a female anime character with spiked hair and monster breasts nearly bursting out of her bodysuit. On the other leg was a tough-looking male character brandishing a sword. For ballpoint on denim, they were definitely works of art.

"What're you starin' at?" Doug said, lifting his chin.

"Nothing," Megan said automatically.

Doug looked down at his jeans and smirked. "Like what you see?"

"Did . . . did you draw those?" Megan asked, trying to make some kind of overture.

"No, brain drain, I let some other mo-fo draw all over my leg at summer school," he said, scrunching his face up.

"Doug! Language!" Regina said.

Doug looked at Megan with clear disdain. "Yo, if you find any of my old *Playboys* in the room, jus' let me know." Then he walked out without a second glance.

"Doug! Douglas Arnold McGowan! Get back here!" Regina called after him. "I'm sorry, Megan."

"It's no problem," Megan said.

As she sat down at the end of the table and poured herself a bowl of cereal, she did her best to relax. Of all the guys in this house, Doug was the one who put her most on edge. She just hoped that if she stayed out of his way, he would stay out of hers.

"This is your school?" Megan asked, staring out through the backseat window of Evan's rusty old Saab.

"This is it," Finn said. "Baker High in all its glory."

"Impressed?" Evan asked.

"Well, kinda," Megan replied.

The building looked like something out of a Harvard brochure. It was an enormous, sprawling redbrick structure with an actual clock tower at the front corner. Huge, shady trees lined the pathways leading up to the main entrance and surrounded the grounds. Dozens of gleaming windows looked out over a babbling brook that ran along the back of the football field. The grass had been clipped so recently it could have been Astroturf, and a huge banner was strung at the top of the bleachers reading *Baker High: Home of the Wildcats.*

Everywhere Megan looked, fresh-faced girls in pleated miniskirts squealed and hugged each other, gushing over their summer memories. A bunch of guys in maroon varsity jackets loitered on the steps in front of the double doors, checking out the scenery. Megan was relieved when she saw a group of girls in jeans walk by, one of them cradling a soccer ball. For a moment, she'd thought she had enrolled in Paris Hilton High.

Evan parked the Saab with a screech of brakes and Megan popped her door open, shouldering her nearly empty backpack. All she had brought with her was her wallet, one notebook, and her soccer cleats, just in case she had a chance to use them. Looking up at the towering building nearly took the breath out of her. Her high school in Texas had been one story of stucco and chrome. This place looked like it had been responsible for the education of the nation's forefathers.

"Come on," Finn said. "We'll show you where the office is."

"Thanks," Megan said.

"You didn't think we were gonna desert you, did ya?" Evan asked, walking backward a few steps and flashing that beautiful grin.

Megan noticed the curious stares of more than a few girls as she walked up the front steps between Evan and Finn. Evan slapped hands with a linebacker type, promising to see him at lunch, and Megan smiled. Walking in with backup was better than walking in alone any day.

"Hey! Strickland!" Evan called the second they walked into

the cozy, trophy-case-packed lobby. "Wait up!" Megan and Finn paused. "Sorry, guys. I gotta do a thing," Evan told them. "I'll catch ya later. Good luck, Kicker."

Evan bounded down a few steps to catch up with his friends. Megan watched him until he reached them, unable to tear her eyes away. They were all athletic types and they were all watching her as Evan slapped hands with them and pounded their backs. When she noticed the attention, she turned away quickly.

"Don't mind him. He needs to greet his people," Finn said with a hint of sarcasm.

"Most popular . . . most athletic . . . most likely to succeed?" Megan asked.

"All of the above," Finn said.

As they walked the halls, Megan noticed that all the lockers were painted maroon and gold and that school spirit banners hung everywhere. Flyers on the walls urged students to sign up for everything from photography club to field hockey to Amnesty International.

"Well, this is it," Finn said, pausing outside a thick wooden door marked *Main Office*. "Don't let old Betsy intimidate you. She's just an unhappy human being."

"Thanks."

"Anytime," Finn said with a half smile, lazily backing away. "Good luck!"

Once Finn was gone, Megan stood in the hallway for a moment, taking it all in. A girl with curly red hair strolled by with her friends and shot Megan a curious but not unfriendly smile.

Here I am again, Megan thought. New town. New school. Surrounded by thousands of new people. She could either let it break her or she could make the best of it.

With a rush of sudden confidence, Megan squared her shoulders. She had done this before, many times. Of course, back then her parents had always been there to rally her when she got home from a bad first day, but she was older now. She could take care of herself. Megan turned on her heel and walked into the office. It was living with seven boys that was going to be challenging. A new school was a piece of cake.

The cafeteria was always the low point. At least in class everyone was all mixed up. Best friends were without their wingmen, cliques without their centers. But in the caf, it all came together. Everyone huddled at their predetermined tables and the new kid was more conspicuous than ever.

Megan walked into the Baker High cafeteria armed with this knowledge and loaded down with more textbooks than any human or pack mule should ever have to carry. Her locker was on the opposite side of the building from every one of her classes, so she hadn't had time to drop anything off. Her mind was spinning with the names of teachers and their assignments, and she was starting to realize that she might really have to bring all this stuff home every single day.

Megan paused near the door and looked around. A few girls had introduced themselves that morning, but no one had made enough conversation to merit crashing their lunch table, and she certainly was not going to horn in on Doug, Finn, or Evan.

She was relieved when she saw that just off the bustling minefield of the standard-issue, double-long tables was a quiet little courtyard dotted with old picnic tables and crooked benches. Only a few random loners sat out there, away from the crowd. It was Megan's utopia.

After choosing a safe-looking deli sandwich, a bag of chips, and a soda from the lunch line, Megan backed through the courtyard door and dropped down at the first empty table.

Shoulders slumped, brain tired, Megan slowly unwrapped her sandwich. All she had to do was get through a couple more classes and then she would be on the soccer field, where she really belonged. She only hoped that the secretary had been right this morning when she'd told Megan that the teams were still taking new-student walk-ons. Betsy didn't seem to be entirely certain about anything except the fact that she was smarter than Megan and everyone else in the room. She had sighed whenever anyone had asked her a question, as if they should already know the answer, but then it had taken her ten minutes to look up the proper response.

"Ah! Here it is!" she had announced, pulling a slip of paper from a folder on her desk. "Coach Leonard is the coach of the girls' soccer team. The team has been practicing since August 20, but new students are welcome to try out. New students should report to the soccer field behind the school on the first day of classes for a tryout."

She lowered her glasses and looked at Megan smugly. "Hope you brought some sneakers with you, dear."

"Never leave home without 'em," Megan replied, patting her backpack.

Now her cleats were tied to the hook strap on her bag to make more room for her many books. She wondered if any of the girls from the team had noticed this in the halls—if they knew she would be coming to practice. She glanced through the window wall into the cafeteria, trying to pick out the girls on the team. Were they any good? Were they *too* good for her to make it?

Megan had a sudden itch for one of her father's patented pep talks. *Too bad he's a few thousand miles away,* she thought, swallowing hard. She was not going to think about her parents. There were a couple more hours to get through and she couldn't be wallowing now.

The door behind her squeaked open and Miller walked out, clutching his tray. His eyes, as always, were riveted on the ground. He made a beeline for the table at the back-right corner of the courtyard, placed his tray down, and sat. He pulled a portable radio out of his black backpack and slipped the headphones over his ears. He happened to look up and saw Megan watching him. For a split second, neither of them moved.

"Hi, Miller," Megan said finally.

"The Yankees are playing their hundred and thirty-fifth game of the season," he replied. Then he flipped a switch and Megan heard the tinny voice of an announcer come to life. He set the radio on the table and went about seasoning his bowl of soup with the plastic salt- and pepper shakers on the table. Megan noticed that his soda can, his bottle of juice, and his snack pack were lined up on his tray in height order. He moved the snack pack over, placed the salt- and pepper shakers between it and the juice bottle, and sat back, satisfied.

TooDamn-Funky: what do u mean funky stuff going on down there??? u cant just say that & not xplain!!!

Kicker5525: OMG This morning Evan woke up and came out of his room with his boxers gaping right open. His cartoon frog boxers.

TooDamn-Funky: OH! HAHAHAHAHAHAHA! u didn't actually c skin, did u?

Kicker5525: OH GOD! No! I didn't look.

TooDamn-Funky: hey! u live in testosteroneville now. get used to it!

Three

The soccer team was gathered on the bleachers when Megan approached. The coach—a tall, muscular woman with short dark hair—had her back to Megan as she spoke with the team. It was a long walk across the field to join them and by the time Megan got there, every one of the players was watching her. She dropped her bag on the bottom step and the coach stopped mid-sentence.

"You must be the new girl I've heard so much about," she said, glancing down at Megan's dirty cleats.

"I guess," Megan said. Apparently she had been right to assume that some of her future teammates would spot her cleats in the hall. "I'm Megan Meade."

"Coach Leonard," she responded. "What position do you play, Megan?"

"Center forward," Megan replied.

Someone blurted a laugh that was followed by a round of others. The whispering that had begun on her arrival intensified and a couple of the girls shook their heads in obvious pity. The coach, however, seemed unfazed.

"All right," she said with a nod. "Girls, why don't we scrimmage and see what Megan can do? Tina, you sit this one out."

Tina, the redheaded girl who had smiled at Megan that morning, grimaced and sat back in her seat while most of the other girls climbed to the ground. She handed Megan a balled-up red vest, which Megan quickly pulled on over her T-shirt.

"Thanks," Megan said.

"Yeah. Break a leg," Tina said sarcastically. So much for that smile.

Megan jogged out to the field and joined the other red shirts on the west side. She greeted the girls on the line and a couple reached out to slap hands with her, but no names were exchanged. Once they got on the field, these girls were all business. Megan liked that.

Coach walked out to midfield with a soccer ball and stepped in between Megan and the opposing center forward. The other girl was tall and tan with broad shoulders, a lean waist, and killer legs. Her blond hair had been highlighted and was pulled into a thick ponytail. She was wearing a little bit too much makeup, but Megan could tell by the fierce look in her eyes that the girl was no Barbie. This was going to be interesting.

The ball dropped, the whistle blew, and it was game on. Megan quickly got control of the ball and started upfield. She passed to the girl on her right and ran ahead, zooming past her first defender, who actually tripped herself up trying to change direction. The ball came back to her seconds later and Megan was rushed hard but deftly popped the ball right through the legs of the halfback. She took the ball downfield, using some fancy footwork to trip up another defender. She raced toward the goal virtually untouched. The goalie, from the look on her face, was completely flummoxed. Megan faked left and kicked right. The girl had no chance.

"Score!" Coach Leonard called out as the ball whizzed into the back of the net.

Megan's teammates crowded around her, slapping her on the back and showering her with high fives. That had been a little too easy. Megan hoped that the starting goalie was at the other end of the field.

"Nice one, Megan!" Coach Leonard called. "The rest of you are making me look bad! Let's go!"

This time the other center forward glowered full force at Megan when they toed the line. "Beginner's luck," she said.

Megan ignored her, knowing she would formulate a come-back five hours from now—one she would never have the guts to deliver anyway. Instead, she'd just make this girl eat her dust.

At the whistle, Megan got the ball again, but this time, Blondie took it right away with a deft, behind-the-legs steal. It happened so fast Megan never saw it coming and she had to laugh as she chased the girl down.

"Nice move," she shouted, impressed.

"Get used to it," the girl replied.

She passed the ball right by Megan, who was two seconds too late to block it. Her teammate took it upfield but quickly lost it. The ball came flying through the air toward Megan. It was a perfect angle for a head pass, so Megan jumped up to take it. But before forehead ever touched leather, she was blindsided—a full-contact hit jarred every bone in her body and threw her to the ground. By the time she looked up again, Blondie was halfway down the field with the ball.

"Watch it, Hailey!" Coach Leonard called out.

"Wow," Megan said under her breath as Hailey scored. "Someone's not messing around."

She knew that Hailey's hit was a blatant foul that probably would have earned her a yellow card in a real game, but Megan liked the fact that the girl wasn't afraid to play rough. Every team needed fearless players like that. And from what she had already seen, Hailey had some of the best moves going.

Maybe even better than mine, Megan thought. Megan was used to being a star on the soccer field, but she knew she'd be okay sharing the spotlight with this girl. She just hoped that Hailey's playing center forward didn't keep her from making the squad.

A few minutes later, the whistle blew and everyone trotted off the field. Megan jogged over to Hailey and put out her hand.

"Nice moves out there," she said. "Never saw you coming."

Hailey looked at Megan's palm like it was covered in ticks. "Yeah, most people don't. That's why I've been All-State for three years in a row and why you'll never get my spot."

Stunned, Megan slowed her steps and let Hailey jog ahead, where she slapped palms with Tina and a few other girls.

"Don't mind Hailey. Nobody likes her."

Another player, the girl who had played right flank on Megan's side, had caught up with her. She had a powerful-looking build, and most of her shoulder-length blond hair had fallen free of its ponytail and now hung in clumps around her clean, sweat-shining face. Megan had noticed her on the field. She was one of the faster girls on the team.

"Not even them?" Megan asked, looking at Hailey's friends.

"She pays them," the girl joked. "As her sister, I get to turn down the money and say what I really think."

"You're *her* sister?" Megan asked, surprised.

"I know. I'm, like, *so* much prettier than her," the girl said, batting her eyelashes comically. "Anyway, I'm Aimee Farmer. Little sister to Hailey 'Queen Bitch' Farmer."

"Ah," Megan said, shaking hands with her. "I'm Megan."

"I know. You were in my chemistry class this afternoon, right?" Aimee asked.

"Oh God. You were there? Sorry, I don't remember anything after I almost burned my lab partner's eyebrows off."

Aimee laughed. "It wasn't that bad. So . . . you were amazing out there. Where did you learn to play like that?"

"I played on a lot of boys' teams growing up," Megan explained as they reached the sideline, where the rest of the team was sucking on their water bottles. "And last year my team was state champion in Texas."

"Wow. Texas. Big state."

"Tell me about it."

"All right, let's run some drills!" Coach Leonard called out. A few girls grabbed the orange cones that were stacked up next to the bleachers and took them back out to the field. "Megan, see me after practice and we'll talk about a spot on the team."

"Sure, Coach," Megan said.

"Depose my sister, please," Aimee said under her breath. "I'll love you forever."

Megan laughed as she and Aimee jogged back onto the field. A familiar and exciting warmth overcame her from head to toe and she relished it, even as she thought with a pang of Tracy and the last time she had felt it. Megan had a feeling she had just made her first new friend.

"Well, Megan, you've got some obvious talent—I don't have to tell you that," Coach Leonard said as they stood in the hallway outside the girls' locker room.

Hair still dripping wet from the shower, Megan crossed her arms over her chest and tried to quell the butterflies inside. She had to make this team. Without the familiarity of soccer practice and drills and games, she would be totally lost.

"But I've already got a starting center forward and she's been my center forward for three years."

Megan gripped herself a little harder.

"So, I have a proposition for you," Coach Leonard said.

"What's that, Coach?" Megan asked hopefully.

"How would you feel about moving over to left forward?" Coach asked. "We're a little weak on that side of the field and I think you'd be a perfect fit."

Megan grinned hugely. "Sure, Coach. Whatever I can do."

"Great," Coach Leonard said, slapping her on the shoulder. "Glad to have you here, Megan. I think with you on board, we could go a long way this year."

"Thanks, Coach."

"See ya tomorrow." Coach Leonard gave Megan a nod as she walked off.

Yes! Thank you, thank you, thank you!

"Hey! You made it?" Aimee asked, noticing Megan's ludicrous grin when she walked out of the locker room a moment later.

"Yep. Left forward," Megan said, hefting her book bag up from the floor, where she had dropped it while talking to the coach. She followed Aimee out into the bright sunshine, feeling lighter than air. She had made the team. Her new life had officially started.

She couldn't wait to get home and tell her mom and dad. *Wait,* call *Mom and Dad,* Megan reminded herself with a serious pang. This had been happening to her all day. Being away from them was going to be hard to get used to. *It's okay. You'll talk to them tonight,* she thought. *It'll be great.*

"Oh, well. So much for the Hailey ego bursting. I was so looking forward to that," Aimee said with a laugh. "But I'm happy for you. Hey . . . you need a ride home?"

"Actually, that would be . . ."

Megan trailed off when she saw a vision that made her lose all power of speech. Evan's car was parked at the curb of the school's driveway and Evan himself was leaning back against it, looking out across the plush front lawn, away from Megan. His legs were crossed at the ankle and his blond hair shone in the sunlight.

He looked up, spotted her, and smiled. He had come to pick her up from practice. There had never been a more perfect moment in all of Megan's life.

But oh God. What was she going to say to him alone in the car for the whole ride home? Sure, he had driven her that morning, but then Finn had been in the front seat with him and the two of them had kept each other occupied. What was she going to do? How was she going to survive this without making a complete idiot of herself?

"Hey, babe!" Evan called out.

Huh?

Hailey jogged past Megan and Aimee, nearly knocking her sister over as she barreled down the pathway and directly into Evan's arms. He lifted her off the ground and mauled her with a long, almost pornographic kiss. Megan couldn't tear her eyes away.

He has a girlfriend, Megan thought, her good mood instantly obliterated. *Of course he has a girlfriend. Just look at the guy.*

But why did it have to be *her*?

"My sister the PDA slut," Aimee said under her breath.

"Get a room!" called one of Hailey's friends from the door behind Megan, earning a round of laughter from the rest of the team.

Hailey detached herself from Evan's face and shot them all a self-satisfied smirk. She took Evan's hand and pulled him away from the car so she could get in. Evan opened the door for her and the moment Hailey's butt hit the seat, she flipped down the visor to check her makeup in the mirror.

"Hey, Megan. You coming?" Evan called out.

Hailey's head snapped up and she glowered out the window.

"Uh . . . yeah," Megan replied, forcing her feet to move. "See you tomorrow," she said to Aimee. She looked at the ground and wrapped her wet hair up into a makeshift bun as she headed for the car. Evan opened the door for her, but she couldn't even look at him as she dropped into the backseat. How could he like Hailey Farmer? He was supposed to be perfect.

"So, how was your first day?" Evan asked as he pulled out of the parking lot.

"It was all right," Megan replied.

"Same old same old," Hailey said at the same time.

Hailey shot Megan a look in the rearview mirror and Evan laughed. "Actually, Hails, I was talking to Megan," he said, reaching out and putting his hand over Hailey's. "We all know how *your* first day went."

He and Hailey exchanged a knowing look and laughed.

"Well, she made the soccer team," Hailey said.

"Cool, Megan. Congrats," Evan said.

"Thanks," Megan said.

"So, where did Coach put you, anyway?" Hailey added. "We know you're not playing center."

Megan's skin burned and she stared out the window.

"I'm playing left," she said.

She saw Hailey's sly smile in the rearview mirror. "Oh, well, left is very important," Hailey said. "You'll be like my wingman."

Megan rolled her eyes and stewed. It was one thing to be comeback-free around a girl like Hailey, but having it happen in front of Evan was ten times worse. Why couldn't she just stick up for herself?

"Don't mind Hailey," Evan said. "Soccer is her life."

Hailey shot Evan an irritated look that he didn't notice. "We're pretty fast up front," she said, glancing over her shoulder. "I hope you can keep up."

"Come on, Hails. Leonard would never have taken her if she wasn't good," Evan said.

Megan could have kissed him. If there weren't a million obstacles, both physical and psychological, in her way, of course.

"I'm just saying," Hailey said, raising her hands. "I just want her to be prepared, that's all."

"Don't worry about me," Megan said. "My team was state champion last year."

There you go! Nice one! she thought, smiling triumphantly.

"Really?" Evan asked, looking over his shoulder. "That's awesome, Kicks."

Megan's smile widened.

"Kicks? What's Kicks?" Hailey asked.

"It's Megan's nickname," Evan said. "Actually, her nickname's Kicker, but I shortened it. I think Kicks is cooler, don't you?" he asked, glancing at Megan in the mirror.

"Definitely," Megan said.

Hailey sat back hard and stared out the window, her jaw set. "That's so nice that you two already have your own nicknames."

"Do I sense a little sarcasm, Hails?" Evan asked playfully. He stopped at a red light, picked up her hand, and kissed it.

Hailey rolled her eyes but smiled. "No," she said. "Not at all. So, how was lacrosse practice? Are you finally going to make All-State this year?"

"You know I don't care about that," Evan said, still holding

Hailey's hand as he turned the wheel with his left. "Lacrosse is for fun. As long as I make first-team hockey—"

"I know! I know! The schools will be coming after *you!*" Hailey replied.

As Evan and Hailey chatted on, Megan found herself suffering from major third-wheel discomfort. She sat back in her seat and gazed out the window, wondering how far Hailey's house was from the school. As much as she didn't want to be left alone in the car to make conversation with Evan, listening to the happy lovers' chatter was much, much worse.

From: Kicker5525@yahoo.com
To: TooDamn-Funky@rockin.com
Sublect: The Immersion Program

Megan Meade's Guide to the McGowan Boys
Entry Two

Observation #1: When there's food in their sights, boys notice little else.

It's like lion-and-gazelle time on Animal Planet. Heidi Klum could walk in and no one would notice. Okay, maybe they would. No way to test that theory. But still, it's like ultimate concentration.

Observation #2: They're easily distracted.

Evan was supposed to show me around school, but he saw some friends and got sidetracked. I chose not to take the slight personally.

Observation #3: They know how to pose.

Evan. His car. Some perfectly placed sunbeams. A casual, unaffected lean. **sigh**

Observation #4: They have bizarro taste in women.

Four

"So, did you have fun?" Regina asked that night as she opened the front door.

"Yeah, thanks again," Megan said. "But you really didn't have to get me all this stuff." Clutched in her hands were four shopping bags full of clothes and makeup Regina had insisted on bringing home for her.

"I didn't have to—I wanted to," Regina said. "Do you know what a pleasure it is to spend time in the women's section at the Gap?"

Megan laughed. "Well, thanks again."

"Anytime," Regina said. "I'm going to make some tea. Do you want some?"

"No thanks. I think I'll just go put all this away."

"Well, good night, hon," Regina said with a smile.

"'Night."

Megan headed down the hallway for the stairs but paused when she heard voices coming from the basement. Down below, Doug called out the play-by-play for what, from the sound of it, was a digital football showdown.

"And Ian's Patriots take the ball on their own thirty-yard line," Doug intoned, lowering his voice to a near-perfect impression of Al Michaels. "Can Ian, the upstart sixth grader, who until recently was still sucking his fruit punch from a sippy cup, beat last year's champion and complete spazmo—all filler, no killer Miller?"

Megan smirked. Doug was actually kind of funny. Who knew?

"And Brady drops back to pass. . . . He's lookin'. . . . He's lookin'. . . ."

Another cheer and Megan heard a couple of high fives. "I don't believe it!" Doug shouted. "Ian's got a first down on the fifty-yard line with a bee-yoo-tee-ful pass to the wide out. He's as cool as the other side a' the pillow. No one saw that comin', especially not Miller's lame-ass defense. If you can even call it that. Ow!"

Apparently Miller had punched Doug. Well deserved. Megan smiled. Part of her wanted to go downstairs and get in on the action, but she didn't want to intrude. Feeling tired and suddenly lonely, Megan started upstairs, the sounds of raucous laughter rising up behind her.

"Regina bought you makeup?" Megan's mother asked over the phone.

"I know, I know. I told her not to, but she insisted," Megan replied, glancing at the half-dozen compacts and tubes on her desk that she was never going to use. Megan just did not consider herself to be a makeup kind of girl. The one time she had let Tracy give her a "light makeover," she had been horrified by the hooker in the mirror and immediately raced for the sink.

"Just don't wear too much of that stuff on your face," her mother said. "You're too pretty for that."

"Thanks," Megan said with a smile. She was proud of her green eyes and her thick, strawberry blond hair, but with her small snub nose, her freckles, and her lack of cheekbones, she had never actually felt "too pretty" for anything.

"Well, I'm sure it's nice for Regina, having another woman around," her mother said. "But I told her she didn't need to buy you anything."

Megan's eyes fell on the Gap and Abercrombie bags on her floor and she cringed. "We didn't buy that much. And I think she really had fun. I mean, *we* had fun," she added. It had been a bit of a marathon spree for Megan—two full hours at the mall playing model—but the Cinnabon had made it all worthwhile.

"Well, good. I'm glad, then," her mother said.

Megan smiled. Talking to her mother wasn't as painful as she had expected it would be. There was a tightness in her chest when she first heard her mom's voice, but she wasn't aching to crawl through the phone line or anything. She took this as a good sign. Maybe she was already getting used to being on her own.

Down the hall a door slammed and Megan flinched. Caleb and Ian were shouting at each other somewhere downstairs. In the attic room over Megan's head, Sean turned on a wailing electric guitar track and flopped down on his bed, the springs squeaking as he settled in.

"Megan?"

"Sorry, Mom. What?" Megan asked.

"Your father wants to know if there's anyone on your soccer team who can keep up with you."

Megan blushed pleasantly. At the same time, she felt a rush of desperate heat, like she would give anything to see her father's face right then. Okay, so maybe this separation wasn't *that* easy.

"One girl's really good," she said. "The rest of them are okay."

There was a quick knock on Megan's door as her mother related this news to her dad.

"Come in," Megan said.

It was Evan. He leaned against the door frame, his hands in his pockets. He was wearing distressed khakis, a white T-shirt, and a perfectly broken-in brown suede car coat.

"Hey," he said.

Holy Abercrombie catalog, Megan thought.

"What? Megan? Did I lose you?"

"Mom, I kinda have to go," Megan said.

"Okay, sweetie," her mother replied. "We'll talk to you soon."

"Okay, Mom. Say 'bye to Dad for me!" she said, swinging her legs around to place her feet on the floor.

"'Bye! Love ya!"

"You too!" Megan replied, turning ten shades of purple. She hung up the cordless phone and tossed it on her bed.

"Hi," she said, attempting a glance at Evan.

"Me and a few of the guys are going out to Logan to watch the planes take off," he said. "Wanna come?"

"Oh . . . uh . . ."

Megan's stomach clenched with nervousness and she looked at

her watch, stalling. He was probably only asking her because his parents had told him to be nice to her or something. Besides, she had school tomorrow. And what if the McGowans got mad at her for going out so late on a school night? As her parents had pointed out about a zillion times, they were doing Megan a huge favor. She didn't want to take advantage of them. It would be so much easier just to plead new-school exhaustion and say she had to go to bed.

"It's kind of late," she said, hating the childish sound of her voice.

"That's kind of the point," he replied. "Come on. It's so cool. And I really want you to meet my friends. You'll love them."

Megan forced herself to look at his face. His perfect face. And he actually looked hopeful. He wasn't messing with her. He really *did* want her there.

"Come on. I know you've got a bad girl in there somewhere," Evan said, flashing his heart-catching smile.

You just could not be more wrong, Megan thought. But she couldn't stop herself from grinning at his words. It was time for her to stop being such a wuss and start taking chances. An image of Ben Palmer popped into her head—the boy she had had a crush on for three full years but never said a coherent word to.

"Okay." She stood up and grabbed her wallet from her dresser. Her pulse was racing so loudly in her ears she could barely hear herself say, "I'm in."

Megan gripped the side of her seat as Evan's car bumped along a dirt road, winding its way through the trees toward the top of a small hill. It wasn't the rough ride or the pitch blackness around her that was making her tense, but the past twenty minutes of stalled conversation—of Evan asking her questions and her coming out with lame non-answers. She had never heard herself say "I don't know" so many times in her life—a phrase she kept repeating just because it was safer than trying to find something cool to say. Megan could not wait to get out of the car.

"So . . . do you miss Texas?" Evan asked, gamely trying to break the silence.

"Kinda," Megan replied.

"Leave anyone behind? Best friends . . . boyfriends . . . ?" Evan asked.

Megan laughed nervously. "No. Well . . . yeah. I mean—"

"Best friend or boyfriend?"

"Best friend. Tracy," Megan said. "No boyfriends."

"Oh. Good."

Megan checked out his profile. He was smiling in a satisfied way. *Please, Megan. He has Hailey. Beautiful, makeup artist, popular, athletic Hailey,* she told herself. *Get a grip.*

Finally they came to a clearing and Megan could see a few cars already parked up ahead. The headlights flashed, illuminating curious faces as Evan parked his Saab. A couple of the guys squinted, then smiled when they saw who was behind the wheel. Hailey jogged away from the crowd, blond hair fanning behind her, and was at Evan's door before he even turned off the engine.

"Hey, baby," she said, grabbing his face through the open window and planting a quick kiss on his lips.

Megan wanted to smack herself. When Evan had mentioned

his friends, she had pictured a bunch of guys. It had never occurred to her that Hailey would be here.

Hailey looked past Evan at Megan. "Oh. Hey," she said flatly.

"Hi," Megan replied. "How's it going?"

"Fine," Hailey said. "You?"

"Fine," Megan replied.

Okay, deep breath, Megan told herself as the dozen or so kids milling around eyed her openly. Megan recognized Tina and another girl from the squad—a pretty, tall Middle Eastern girl with dark curly hair. Evan and Hailey walked around to Megan's side of the car, arms around each other.

"Everyone! This is Megan," Evan called out. "Megan, this is everyone."

"Hi, Megan!" they all trilled, like a class full of kindergarteners.

Megan laughed and lifted her hand. "Hi."

"I'll go get us a couple of beers," Evan said to Hailey. "You want?" he asked Megan.

"No thanks."

"Be right back," Evan said. Then he jogged off toward his friends, leaving Megan and Hailey standing together. Megan felt like she could breathe again. She looked at Hailey out of the corner of her eye.

Maybe Hailey was just threatened this afternoon. After all, you are a great soccer player and you are a girl who's living with her boyfriend. But you have a lot in common with her. Maybe there's still a chance for you to get along.

"So, Hailey, what was the team's record last year?" she asked.

"We won more than we lost," Hailey said, pushing her hands into the front pockets of her tight jeans. "Why? Worried the team's not good enough for you?"

Megan stared at her. "No. I'm just making conversation."

"Well, we made it to counties, but we didn't win the final," Hailey said. "Of course, Coach thinks that with you around, it'll happen this year."

"Thanks," Megan said.

"I said, 'Coach thinks.'"

At that moment, a plane took off from the runway and skimmed just above their heads, its wheels hanging so low Megan thought it might hit one of the trees behind them. The roar was deafening. Megan could see that Evan and his friends were cheering at the top of their lungs, fists and beer cans raised to the air, but she couldn't hear them. Megan wanted to scream too—at Hailey. In her mind she heard Tracy telling her to stick up for herself. If she could stand up to her parents, she could certainly stand up to this girl. But just the thought made her palms sweat and her heart pound.

I have to do something, though, Megan thought, trying to pep-talk herself. *She's going to walk all over me if I don't do something.*

As soon as the engine noise had faded, Megan turned to Hailey again.

"Can I ask you a question?"

"What?"

"Did I do something? I mean, to offend you?" Megan asked. "All I'm trying to do is settle in at a new school, maybe make some friends, play a little soccer. But you seem to really not like me."

Megan held her breath, unable to believe that her thoughts had actually come out in a semi-coherent way. For a split second, Hailey's face softened and Megan realized that the girl was really pretty when she didn't have her scowl on. She even looked like she was going to say something semi-human. Then Evan broke away from the crowd with his beers and Hailey saw him coming. She glanced at Evan, then at Megan, and reached out her arm to him.

"Come on, baby," she said, latching onto his side. "Let's go find someplace a little more private."

"Cool," Evan said, handing Megan one of the beers. "Go introduce yourself around, Kicks. The guys are dying to meet you," he added with a wink.

"Oh . . . kay."

She watched helplessly as Hailey led Evan away and the group behind her laughed loudly at some unheard joke. Hailey glanced over her shoulder, shooting Megan a triumphant look before she and Evan ducked into the trees.

"Okay, so what do we got so far? In Boston we got trees, we got water, we got the Red Sox, we got the aquarium, and we got the . . . We got the . . ."

Megan looked at Darnell Wilcox. He had ticked off his list on his fingers and was now staring down at his pinky as if it were going to give him the answer. In the other hand he clutched the neck of a half-empty bottle of Budweiser—from what Megan could tell, his fifth or sixth. Darnell was a handsome guy who, according to his varsity jacket, was captain of the football team. At the beginning of the night, he had shown himself to be a smart, friendly, funny guy. Now that he was officially drunk, he was still friendly and funny, but the smart thing was out the window.

"History," Megan said. "You forgot history."

"Right!" Darnell said, his big brown eyes lighting up as he looked at her. "Now, what kinda history you got in Texas?"

Megan leaned back on the hood of Darnell's old-school Corvette and sighed. "Oh, I don't know, we've got Coronado, the Alamo. . . . We declared independence once," she said, glancing at him.

Darnell stared at her for a second, his eyes scrunched in confused surprise, as if her sound track had switched over to SAP. "Yeah, well, we got the Boston Tea Party, the Boston Massacre, the Boston . . . the Boston . . ."

"Red Sox!" someone shouted, prompting a round of cheers in the darkness.

"Yes! Thank you!" Darnell said, raising his bottle. "The Boston Red Sox . . ."

"You mentioned them already," Megan said with a yawn.

"Oh, sorry," Darnell said slurrily. "Am I boring you?"

"No." Megan shook her head. He was actually quite entertaining. It was just that it was past midnight and the night was getting old.

"Yeah . . . well, I'm boring myself," Darnell said, lying back next to her.

Together they stared up at the sky as yet another plane whooshed by. Everyone else cheered, but Megan squeezed her eyes closed and covered her ears against the noise.

"Hey. You guys having fun?"

Megan opened her eyes to find Evan hovering over her. Sweet relief! She hadn't seen him since Hailey had dragged him off two hours ago. Now they could finally get out of here.

"You ready to go?" Megan asked, sliding down off the hood of the car. She glanced at Hailey, noticed a throbbing hickey right near her collarbone, and glanced away. Her heart burned with jealousy. She didn't even want to imagine where else Evan's lips had been. But now, of course, she couldn't help it.

"Already?" Hailey asked, reaching for Evan's hand with both of hers. "I've barely even talked to anybody."

Yeah? And whose fault is that? Megan thought.

Evan shot Megan a pleading look and Megan's spirits dropped. Suddenly she felt even more exhausted than she had a second ago.

"You know what? That's fine," Megan said, grabbing Darnell's hand and pulling him into a seated position. His eyes rolled forward and he attempted to focus. "I'll just have Darnell here drive me home. You're okay to drive, right, Darnell?" she asked, slapping him on the back so hard he slid off the car.

He stumbled a second when his feet hit the ground, but he fished his keys out of the pocket of his varsity jacket. "Toad-al-ly," he said. "Jus . . . tell me where ya live."

He aimed the keys for the lock in the door and hit the window.

Megan raised her eyebrows at Evan. Evan looked back,

amused and clearly somewhat impressed. Megan could barely believe it herself. She was actually standing up to him. Who would have thought it was possible?

They both knew she wasn't stupid enough to get into the car with Darnell. It was a bluff. The question was, what would Evan do?

He turned to Hailey. "Maybe we should go."

Megan's heart fluttered like a victory flag in the wind.

Hailey's face fell, but she recovered quickly. "Fine. I'll go get my bag. You can drop me off."

"Actually . . . do you think you could maybe drive Darnell home?" Evan asked, pressing his lips together and raising his eyebrows adorably.

They all looked over at Darnell's stooped figure as he used two hands to guide his key toward the lock. He missed again.

"Evan—"

"Hails, you live two houses down from him," Evan said. "And somebody's gotta do it."

Hailey looked over her shoulder at the others as another plane took off and drowned out the world. "Okay, you're right," she said with a sigh. She walked over to Darnell and slung her arm around his broad back. "Wrong side of the car, D."

"Huh?" Darnell said. "But I'm driving Megan home."

"Change of plans. You've got me now," Hailey said. "Come on."

Megan watched as Hailey gently led Darnell around to the passenger seat. Evan took the keys and opened the door. Together they lowered Darnell's linebacker frame into the car. Then Hailey fished around under the seat and adjusted it so that

Darnell's knees weren't pressed into the dashboard. Unreal. Just when Megan thought the girl was completely evil, she went and acted like a human.

"Okay, see you later," Hailey said, giving Evan a kiss before she got behind the wheel.

"Drive safe," Evan replied, coaxing a smile out of his girlfriend.

"Bye, Hailey," Megan said as Hailey started the car.

Without another word, Hailey peeled out, leaving Megan and Evan in the dust.

"Nice girl," Megan said under her breath.

Evan looked at her sideways and turned toward his car. "Come on. Let's go home."

"So, are your parents going to kill us?" Megan asked, checking her watch. One-fifteen a.m. "'Cuz my parents would definitely kill us."

"Don't worry. It's under control," Evan said.

He turned off the headlights as he turned onto the McGowans' quiet street. Parking his car at the very end of the driveway, he cut the engine. The sound of a hundred chirping crickets filled the air. The only light in the house came from the lamp in the front living room window.

"Hey," Evan whispered. "Did you have fun tonight?"

Megan turned to look at him, her heart responding with a heavy thump. He was leaning across the center console. Leaning so close she could see the stubble coming in on his jawline.

"Your friends are nice."

"I knew you would like them," he whispered, looking into

her eyes so intently, she couldn't look away. "Actually I knew they would like you."

Megan swallowed with difficulty. "You . . . you did?"

"Well, what's not to like?" Evan said with a smile.

Oh God, he was going to kiss her. He was going to kiss her right there in the driveway. And she so, *so* wanted him to. She wanted him to so much she could feel it in every last molecule of her body.

But he has a girlfriend, Megan, she told herself. Hailey might be a bitch, but she was a girl and a teammate and, although the opportunity had never presented itself before, Megan was not the type of person who stole other people's boyfriends, no matter how hateful those people were.

"Okay, just close . . ."

Megan couldn't move.

". . . your door very quietly," Evan whispered.

He turned and got out of the car. Megan deflated.

She slipped out of the car and closed the door. Noiselessly she followed Evan up the driveway and along the side of the house. Aside from the crickets, all Megan could hear was the sound of her own breathing. Every other second she expected a window to open above them or a light to flick on, but everything was still. Evan really seemed to know what he was doing.

He reached the back door and opened the screen door halfway, stopping it with the toe of his suede sneaker. "Lesson one," he whispered. "If you only open it this far, it doesn't squeak."

Megan smiled. "Got it."

He bent down and lifted the welcome mat to reveal a single

key. "Lesson two: Using this key is a lot quieter than pulling out your whole key chain."

Megan held her breath as Evan unlocked the door. He dropped the key under the mat again and tilted his head, telling Megan to go in ahead of him. For a long moment, Megan paused, staring at the slim space between Evan and the door frame.

She had to turn sideways to get by him. As she slid into the house, her entire body brushed against his. Leg to leg, chest to chest, her cheek tilted just under his nose so that she could feel his hot breath on her face. She expected him to move slightly, to give her more room, but he didn't.

Megan finally stepped free. She couldn't stop grinning as the cool, open air of the kitchen whooshed over her, heightening the tingling warmth all over her skin. Evan turned his back to her as he quietly closed and locked the door. The house was deathly silent.

"Back stairs," he whispered.

His voice sent shivers all through her body. Megan tiptoed behind him. He stopped at the bottom of the steps to let her go by and her heart pounded with anticipation. She put her foot on the first stair and paused, realizing she needed to say something—that she somehow felt that she might actually be able for-mulate a sentence. Maybe even say something cool.

This was her chance. She had to take it.

She turned abruptly and Evan walked right into her.

"Oh!" he said. He stumbled, placed his foot back on the floor again for balance, and clutched the wall. They both laughed and slapped their hands over their mouths. Megan relished the moment, laughing along with Evan, alone and forbidden in his darkened house.

"What?" he asked, his brown eyes sparking in the dim moonlight. "What is it?"

"I just . . . I just wanted to say thanks. You know, for taking me out tonight," Megan said. "It was . . . very cool of you."

Evan smiled and looked deeply into her eyes. He leaned forward and Megan found she couldn't breathe. This was it. *This* was *definitely* it. And suddenly she wasn't even thinking about Hailey or the fact that half an hour ago he had been making out with someone else. All she could think about was the fact that she *really* wanted to kiss him. And that she should try to intake some oxygen. If this was going to be her first kiss, she didn't want to faint on him. Megan's eyes fluttered closed as Evan leaned closer and closer. Then, ever so softly, he touched her cheek. She felt him move away and she opened her eyes. He was holding out a fingertip to her.

"Eyelash," he whispered. "Make a wish."

Megan's heart quickened. She bit her lip, made her wish, and blew.

"What's going on?" The stairwell flooded with light.

"Dad!"

"Am I dreaming or is it after one in the morning?" John said from above. There was a bend in the stairs, so they couldn't see him, but Megan could tell how pissed off he was from the timbre of his voice.

"*Crap,*" Evan said under his breath.

"Just digging the hole deeper, Ev," his father said.

"Oh God," Megan whispered, covering her eyes.

"Both of you get to your rooms," John said. "We'll discuss this tomorrow."

"Sorry," Evan mouthed to Megan.

"Now," John said.

And with that, Evan brushed past her and jogged up the stairs.

From: Kicker5525@yahoo.com
To: TooDamn-Funky@rockin.com
Subject: Boy Guide

Megan Meade's Guide to the McGowan Boys
Entry Three

Observation #1: Boys are very stealthy when they want to be. Evan has all kinds of tricks for sneaking back into the house after hours. (I know you're dying to know why I know this.)

Observation #2: Boys lose their cool when snagged by their parents.
Once inside the house, Evan is not so stealthy. Of course, maybe if he hadn't stopped on the stairs to brush the eyelash off my cheek and have me make a wish, we would never have gotten caught. (Ahhhhhhh!!!!)

Observation #3: Boys have one-track minds.
Unfortunately, Evan's train is not on MY track. (I know, major letdown.) But who knows? Maybe his train will be making an unscheduled stop in Meganville. ☺

Okay, sorry. No more metaphors this late at night. I promise.

Five

Megan sat back in the window seat after practice on Wednesday and stared at the list of sites about Asperger's syndrome on Google. For a disorder she had never heard of until yesterday, there sure was a lot of information out there. She clicked on the first site and started to read.

Downstairs, Sean's band was playing some disorganized tune that sounded vaguely familiar. Megan was on edge, expecting every second to hear a knock on the door, waiting for the judgment to be handed down.

Asperger's syndrome is a developmental disorder characterized by sustained impairment of social interaction and the development of repetitive patterns of interests, behaviors, and activities, Megan read. That sounded about right. But what to do to make Miller comfortable around her? She scrolled down through causes and comparisons to autism and finally found a section she could use. "Living with Asperger's."

The back door slammed and Megan cracked the blinds slightly so she could see out the window. Finn walked across the yard and into the toolshed on the far side. Megan watched and waited for him to come out, wondering what he needed back there. She waited. And waited. No Finn. Why was he hanging out in the toolshed?

"Mom! Mom! Ian's sitting on my Patriots hat and he won't let me have it back!" Caleb shouted at the top of his lungs.

"It's my hat! No one said you could have it!" Ian shouted back.

"Yuh-huh! Dad did! He said you outgrew it, fathead!"

Megan stifled a laugh.

"Ian! Caleb! Get down here!" John bellowed, cutting the argument short. "In fact, all of you, in the living room! Someone get Finn out of the backyard, please. We're having a family meeting."

Megan's heart stopped beating and she froze. Maybe if she didn't make a noise, they would forget she was here. There was a general grumbling among the boys, but from the sounds in the hallway, they were all trailing out of their rooms and down the stairs. The music from the garage was cut dead with a crash of cymbals and Miller went outside to get Finn. Apparently these family meetings were serious business.

For a long, bizarre moment, Megan was enveloped by complete and utter silence. And then it happened.

"Megan? Would you join us, please?" John called.

Megan closed her eyes. Setting her computer aside, she took a deep breath and headed downstairs. From just a few steps down she could see the entire living room and all the boys sitting on the U-formation couches like they were waiting at a doctor's office.

She glanced at Evan, who was looking right at her. Somehow he managed to shrug with his eyes, like, "What can you do?"

Megan tromped down the last few stairs, feeling everyone watching her. Regina and John stood in front of the fireplace, facing their sons. There was a space saved between Finn and Doug on the big couch in the center. A quick glance around the room told her that was exactly where she fit in heightwise. Apparently Miller was in charge of the seating arrangements.

"Megan, would you sit next to Finn, please?" Regina asked.

"Sure," Megan said, wiping her palms on her jeans.

She squeezed uncomfortably into the tight spot and Doug made an elaborate shift, turning his knees away from her so that no part of his body was touching any part of hers. His move only pressed her farther into Finn's side.

"Sorry," she said, blushing.

Finn cleared his throat. "No problem," he said.

He lifted his arm and laid it on the back of the couch, giving them both a little more room. Megan tucked her arms in front of her and crossed her legs tightly, making her body as small as possible. She hoped the meeting was quick, because she wasn't going to be moving a muscle.

"Okay, I'm sure you all know why we're here," John began. "Your mother and I know that you guys are all doing your best to make Megan feel welcome."

Doug let out a grunt that only Megan could hear and Finn shifted slightly, pressing himself into the arm of the couch. Megan's heart pounded a mile a minute.

"Now, we were hoping we weren't going to have to have this

conversation. We were hoping we could trust you guys to set a good example," John continued. "But Evan's behavior last night has forced our hand."

"Nice one, loser," Doug said.

Megan blushed furiously. Doug pulled out a pen, uncapped it with his teeth, and started to add to the doodle on his jeans— the same ones he had worn the day before.

"Now, in case any of you knuckleheads were having any funny ideas about the new member of the household, your mother and I have one thing to say," John continued. "As far as you all are concerned, Megan is not a girl."

Doug cackled and Megan sank down in her seat. She stared at a knot in the center of the wood floor.

"Then what is she?" Caleb asked innocently, making Doug and a couple of the others laugh.

"Caleb," Regina said softly, scoldingly. "What your father is trying to say is, while Megan is living with us, you guys are to treat her like a sister. You all are brothers and sister, got it?"

Megan was dying to look at Evan. Instead her eyes darted right and landed on Ian, who was blowing gum bubbles. Then she managed a glance at Sean, who was looking at his watch. Finally, with the effort of ten men, Megan managed to find Evan. He was staring straight ahead, his heels tapping an unsteady beat on the floor.

"Megan?" John said.

She turned and looked at John.

"What?" she asked.

"Do you understand?" John asked.

"Oh. Yes, sir."

"And the rest of you?" John asked.

"Yeah, hands off Megan. We got it," Doug said. "Can we go now?"

"Wait! Does that include Caleb?" Ian asked, cracking up at his own joke.

"Nice one, wise guy," Regina said. "You just got yourself trash duty for a week."

Doug started to get up.

"We're not done yet," his father said. Doug flopped back down with a huge sigh.

"I know you're all used to having the run of the house around here, but that changes now," John said, raising his voice slightly. "Megan's parents have entrusted us with her care, and that means all of us. As of right now, you will all start respecting her privacy. That means no going into her room without permission, not touching her things, and from now on, the oak tree out back is off-limits."

"No fair!" Caleb cried.

"That's the climbing tree!" Ian added.

"Not anymore," his father said. "And we're going to have a curfew."

"What? That's crap!" Doug blurted. "Sean never had a curfew!"

"Well, things were different when Sean was in high school," Regina said.

"Yeah, *Kicker* the buzz kill wasn't here," Doug said.

"You want a week of trash?" John asked, his eyes flashing.

Oh God. They're going to kill me. They're all going to kill me, Megan thought.

"The new curfew is midnight," John said, gazing sternly at each of his sons in turn. "And don't think that your mother and I aren't going to enforce it. You think you've been grounded before, just test me. A new day has dawned, guys. Get used to it."

"Dad!" Evan said, sitting forward.

"Trust me, Ev, you're the last one who should try to argue with me on this," his father said firmly.

"Thanks a lot," Doug said under his breath.

Finn smacked him on the back of the head as Megan prayed for the sweet relief of death. If these guys hadn't despised her before, they definitely did now.

"All right, everyone," Regina said, clapping. "Let's eat."

That night Megan scrubbed her face vigorously with the exfoliating apricot face wash Regina had left for her in her bedroom. It seemed that Regina was going to continue to try to put Megan in touch with her girly side whether she wanted to be or not. But that was the least of Megan's problems—Evan hadn't even looked at her once during dinner and Doug had kept kicking her foot away under the table. And every time someone passed a dish to Megan, Ian had shouted, "Hands off!" and cracked up laughing. The whole experience had been completely humiliating.

Everything's going to be fine, she told herself, staring into her own eyes in the mirror. Unfortunately, she didn't quite believe it. The McGowans had just put the nix on any possibility of Megan and Evan getting together, however remote it had been.

Plus they had apparently made Doug hate her even more—something she hadn't thought possible. At least John, at Regina's urging, had put locks on her bedroom and the bathroom. Otherwise she might wake up one night to find Doug getting ready to smother her with a pillow.

Megan splashed water on her face and turned off the faucet. *Hmm. Okay, so this actually smells pretty good.* As she pressed a towel to her skin, she heard voices on the other side of the wall and paused. They were coming from Evan's room.

"This sucks," someone whispered. "Since when are they so big on us following the rules?"

"One guess," another voice replied.

Megan shivered and wrapped her arms around herself. She tiptoed over to the toilet seat and sat down to listen.

"Look, I've never seen Mom and Dad that serious," someone else said. "You monkeys better get ready for a big-time crackdown."

"We had this place wired tight, yo," Doug said. "Now the girl has scorched that. I say we ice her until she cracks. We make it so bad she'll be beggin' to jet to Korea."

Megan swallowed hard. Wasn't anyone going to defend her? Finn? Evan? Anyone?

"Did you know that the Yankees have appeared in thirty-nine World Series and have won twenty-six of them?"

Megan smiled sadly.

"Yeah, we know that, dill hole," Doug snapped. "But who won in 2004?"

"The Red Sox. But—"

"And who did they kick the big, fat butts of to get there?" Doug asked.

"The Yankees, but—"

"Then why don't you just shut up?"

Megan took a deep breath. She slipped her towel over the towel bar and took a good, long look at herself in the mirror. If someone set a challenge like this in front of her on the soccer field, it would be rally time. But seven-to-one odds were not good. These guys not only had home field advantage, but they had their own language, their own history, their own secret playbook. Megan was going in blind.

You should just walk in there. Shock the hell out of them. Tell them that you heard everything and that they're not going to run you out of here without a fight, Megan told herself. But of course she would never do that.

As the conversation next door degenerated into a sports debate, Megan turned away from her reflection. She was starting to wonder if coming to live with the McGowans was the worst mistake of her life.

From: Kicker5525@yahoo.com
To: TooDamn-Funky@rockin.com
Subject: Boy Guide

Megan Meade's Guide to the McGowan Boys
Entry Four

Observation #1: Boys don't know when to keep it down.

Six

Megan wrapped her still-damp hair back in a ponytail and pulled her red hoodie over her head. The sun was still pink in the morning sky and the first sounds of stirring could be heard from the boys' rooms. She snagged her backpack, stuffed her feet into her sneakers, and headed for the stairs on her tiptoes.

The kitchen was dark and silent, just as she had hoped it would be. She yanked open the door to the cupboard and stepped inside. The place was stocked like a bomb shelter. Twelve boxes of cereal, at least fifty cans of soup, rows and rows of macaroni-and-cheese boxes, crackers, cookies, and jumbo bags of pretzels. Regina and John must have to go shopping every day to keep their little brood of demons fed.

Megan scanned the shelves, found an open box of granola bars, and grabbed two. Then she snagged a fruit punch Gatorade from the fridge and headed out the back door. Nothing like breakfast on the run.

Her bike was parked with half a dozen others under a metal awning that stretched out from the side of the shed. Putting a wrapped granola bar between her teeth, she extricated the handlebars from the others and walked her bike to the driveway. She slipped the Gatorade bottle into the bottle holder, hopped on, and pedaled toward school. She only hoped that after two rides in the back of Evan's car, barely paying attention to where she was going, she would somehow remember the route.

Fifteen minutes later, Megan popped the curb and rode over the grass, right up to the bike rack at the front of the school. Kids were already arriving and a few clumps of people stood outside, chatting or looking over each other's notes. Megan tore open the second granola bar and took a nice long drink from the Gatorade bottle as she walked up the steps. She was feeling good—independent. Who needed the McGowan boys? She could take care of herself. From the corner of her eye, she saw Hailey and her friends watching her as she reached the top step.

"So . . . *Kicker*," Hailey said with a smile. "I see you're no longer using my boyfriend as your chauffeur."

Megan was not in the mood. She paused for a long moment and stared at Hailey straight in the eye until Hailey's face finally fell. Then she looked at the other girls who had smiled at the joke and let her eyes slide over them. There were two girls who hadn't laughed or reacted. Megan smiled at those two before biting into her granola bar and striding past them into the building.

Miller was already sitting at his table in the courtyard when Megan walked out with her lunch tray that afternoon. One thing Megan had learned on the Web was that if Miller was ever going to be comfortable with her around, she was going to have to let him see that she was here to stay—that she was someone he needed to get used to. While avoiding the other boys seemed like a good plan, hanging with Miller was the only way to help him. Now was as good a time as any to start.

She didn't want to invade his personal space, so she sat down across the table from him and at the other end, as far away as possible. Through his headphones, she could hear an announcer calling a game, rambling on about the pitch count. Miller looked up and stared at her, his eyes blank. Flushing under his unabashed gaze, Megan looked down at her tray. She began lining up the items in front of her in height order. Soda can, apple, mini–ketchup bottle, fruit cup. The burger and fries she kept right in front of her. When she was finished, she looked up at Miller again and he smiled.

He had a great smile. It lit up his entire face. Megan smiled back and Miller returned to his lunch. Megan took a big bite of her hamburger as a shadow fell across her meal. She looked up to find Evan standing at the end of her table. Her cheek was stuck out chipmunk style. She groped for a napkin and covered her mouth while she finished chewing.

"How's it going?" Evan asked, sliding into the chair across from hers. He had no bag, no books, no lunch. "Hey, Mills," he said, nodding at his brother.

Miller lifted his hand and turned up the volume on his radio.

"It's pretty cool, you know. You sitting out here with him," Evan said.

In the sunlight she could see that his brown eyes had these amazing gold flecks that made them sparkle. But she couldn't get sucked in. She refused.

"Why don't you guys sit with him?" Megan asked, leaning back and crossing her arms over her chest. Somehow Evan didn't seem as nerve shaking as he had the night before.

"You know how it is," Evan said with a shrug. "So, what happened to you this morning? You left."

"Yep," Megan said flatly. "I left."

There was a long pause and someone on the radio hit a home run.

"You heard us last night, didn't you?" Evan said, hunching forward with his hands clasped between his knees.

Megan cast a look at him that showed him she had heard everything. Evan's head fell.

"You know what? It's fine," Megan said, grabbing a french fry. "I'll just keep to myself. . . . I won't bother anybody . . . and you all will just forget I'm even there."

"Yeah, bad idea," Evan said.

"Excuse me?" Megan said, her face heating up.

"Look, ignoring my brothers is not the answer," Evan said. "Trust me. I've lived with them a little longer than you have. You ignore them, they'll just turn the screws even harder."

"Oh."

"I mean, you *can't* ignore us," Evan added. "In case you haven't noticed, we're kind of everywhere."

Megan snorted a laugh, then tried to cover it by taking a loud slurp of soda.

"You can't let them think they can walk all over you, 'cuz they will," Evan said. "The in-their-face tactic is pretty much the only thing they respond to."

Megan chewed on the rim of her soda can.

"Megan? Are you in there?" Evan asked, waving a hand in front of her face.

Megan nodded and sat forward, placing her can back down on the tray. "I'll try," she said, staring at the tray. "Thanks." She looked up at him. "I mean, for the advice."

"Yeah, no problem," Evan said, grabbing a fry from her tray. "I still can't believe my parents, you know? With that curfew? I bet your parents never gave you a curfew."

Megan shrugged. Her parents had never needed to give her a curfew. She always came home on her own, way earlier than any self-respecting teenager should ever be home.

"Whatever. Screw them," Evan said. "Sean never had a curfew; why should I? They think you're here and now suddenly we need rules?" He scoffed and took another french fry. "I'm not gonna be following any of them."

Megan's pulse raced and she stared at his mischievous smile. When he said he wasn't going to be following any of the rules, did that include the "hands off Megan" rule?

"You know what? It's a good fry day. I'm gonna go get something to eat," he said.

"Oh. Okay. I'll . . . see you later."

Evan looked at her, perplexed. "I'll go get something to eat and then come back," he said slowly, like he was talking to someone who had just learned English.

"Oh," Megan said, smiling. "Okay."

He walked through the door and Megan followed him with her eyes, a goofy grin plastered to her face. Evan was going to eat lunch with her. By choice. This had to mean something. And unless she was wrong, they had just had an actual conversation with only one little snort to speak of. This day was looking up.

As Megan returned to her lunch, something inside the cafeteria caught her eye. Hailey was glaring at her. She was sitting at a table in the center of the room and she and all her friends were openly, blatantly glaring at her.

Megan's stomach churned and she averted her eyes quickly, pretending not to have noticed. Unbelievable. Why was Evan going out with someone who was obviously so bitchy? He deserved so much better. Megan picked up her hamburger and took a big bite.

From now on, it's every woman for herself, Megan thought. Then she giggled at her sudden boldness, grabbed her school-issue copy of *Hamlet* from her backpack, and buried her flushed face in its pages.

The sun beat down on Megan's back as she took the ball up the sideline. She was working on pure adrenaline. Blood dripped from a scrape on her knee, soiling her sock and the cushioning on her shin guard. Her arm was streaked with dirt and her nose was on the verge of running. Still, all Megan cared about was the feel of the wind blowing her hair back as she raced down the field. All she could see was the goal in front of her. All she could sense was Hailey breathing down her neck. The girl was right on her heels.

Megan set up to pass, but at the last second, something caught her ankle and she flew off her feet. Her forward motion was helped by a swift shove between her shoulder blades and Megan's head snapped backward as the rest of her body slammed into the ground. It hurt like hell, but she didn't stay down for long. She was not going to let Hailey get the best of her, no matter how many illegal tackles the girl flattened her with.

"Hailey! What the hell are you doing?" Ria Wilkins shouted, offering her arm to Megan.

Ria was a compact, powerful defensive player. She and Aimee had gotten Megan's back all day, taking some of the burden off her once they realized that Hailey was going to try to kill Megan every time Megan got the ball.

"What?" Hailey said, stopping and popping the ball up to her hands. "I'm just doing my job."

"Please! You totally shoved her down!" Aimee countered.

"You guys, it's fine," Megan said, sucking wind. "It was a clean play."

"It was not and you know it," Ria replied. "I'm sorry, but where I come from, you get a kick-ass player on your team, you don't try to sideline her at practice."

"What are you saying, Ria?" Hailey asked, getting up in Ria's face. "Are you saying I don't care about this team?"

"Hey, you said it, not me," Ria replied, staring at Hailey.

Suddenly the whistle started bleating furiously and Coach Leonard broke into the center of the rapidly growing circle. Megan stepped aside and wiped the back of her hand under her nose. Hailey had been fairly violent today, but Megan had given as good as she had gotten. Megan's hits had been clean, unlike Hailey's, but Hailey had eaten plenty of turf herself. Her elbow was banged up and her face was streaked with grass and dirt. It was all part of the game.

"All right, girls, that's it. I think we're calling practice a little early today," Coach Leonard said, glaring at all of them. "I like the energy I'm seeing out here, but Hailey, Megan, if you two don't clean up your act and do it fast, the refs will be sidelining you before you can say O and ten," she added, glancing at both of them. "We're not gonna be winning much without you two on the field, so I suggest you start finding a way to work together."

"Yes, Coach," Megan said quickly.

"Yes, Coach," Hailey added.

"Good. Now before you hit the showers, I want to remind you all that at our last Saturday practice before the game against Hacketstown, we're going to be electing our new captain," Leonard said. "So start thinking about what kind of person you want to have leading this team."

Almost everyone looked at Hailey. Clearly the girl had a lock on the captainship. Megan thought of her team back in Texas— the team she was supposed to captain this year. She took a deep breath and let it out slowly, trying to ignore the pang of regret in her chest.

"All right, let's hit the showers," Coach Leonard said.

The group broke up and Vithya Jane, the girl Megan had recognized at Logan the other night, came over and slapped her hand. "Nice practice," she said.

"Thanks," Megan replied, surprised that any friend of Hailey's would give her props.

Vithya smiled and jogged to catch up with Hailey and Tina while Aimee and Ria flanked Megan.

"We should clean up that knee," Ria said, wincing as she looked at the blood.

"Eh, I kind of like it," Megan said. "It's my first Wildcat battle scar."

Aimee and Ria laughed and the three of them chatted all the way back to the gym.

Megan was sure she was fine until she stepped off her bike in the McGowans' driveway and her muscles cramped up. Apparently she was due for a bit more stretching. Hailey had really given her the workout of a lifetime that afternoon. If the girl didn't watch out, she was going to wind up improving Megan's game instead of putting her on the injured list.

The back door closed as Megan came around the house, and she saw Finn cross the yard and head into the toolshed again. Megan wheeled her bike over to the side wall and propped it up with the others. She paused for a moment, listening. There was no noise. Nothing. What was he doing in there?

God, I really hope it doesn't involve a stack of Playboys *or something,* Megan thought, grimacing.

Still, even with that disgusting thought in her mind, she couldn't help giving in to her curiosity. Besides, she was supposed to be immersing. Part of that was finding out what guys did when they were by themselves in a toolshed, right?

Bracing herself, Megan walked over to the door and pulled it open. Finn whirled around, his eyes wide, and stared at her. He was wearing a blue T-shirt that read *Good Boys Vote* and it was dotted with fingerprints of purple paint. His hair was a little more mussed than usual.

"Okay, life flashing before my eyes," he said, letting out a breath. "You scared the crap outta me."

"Sorry," Megan said.

Something in her mind told her that she should just back out of the room, but she was too stunned to move. Finn was not, thank goodness, doing anything unsavory. He was holding a paint palette and a brush and standing in front of a canvas. Around him, behind him, on the floor, and leaning against the walls were dozens of other canvases, all in various stages of completion. None, as far as she could tell, were finished.

"Wow," Finn said, looking her up and down. "Wander into a bad part of town?"

Megan looked down at the scrape on her left knee and the nasty bruise forming on her shin.

"No. It was . . . practice," Megan said. "I'm sorry, should I go?"

"No! No," Finn said, pulling a stool out from the wall. "Come in. Take a load off. You look like you could use it."

Megan smiled and inched into the shed, afraid to touch anything with any part of her body. She slipped sideways past his easel and sat down on the stool, which shifted under her weight. Megan threw her arms out for balance and Finn caught her hand.

"Sorry. It's kind of old," he said.

"No problem," Megan replied. She looked at his hand

clamped around hers. He released her, clearing his throat and slapping his palm against his jeans.

"So, Hailey give you those?" Finn asked, lifting his chin and looking at her legs. He squirted some paint from a tube onto his palette and pressed his brush into it, mixing it around.

"How did you know?" Megan asked.

"I know Hailey," Finn replied, blowing away a blond curl that fell in front of his eye. "At the Fourth of July party at the town pool in second grade, she stole my Popsicle and shoved me into the deep end. I've been afraid of her ever since."

"Seriously?" Megan said with a smirk.

"I never joke about Popsicles," Finn replied with a half smile.

Megan laughed and looked around. The half-finished painting nearest to her showed a pair of hands, one laid across the other in a graceful pose. The fingers, however, hadn't been detailed and they tapered off into nothing. Behind that was what appeared to be the bare shoulder and neck of a girl who was half looking away from the viewer, but her hair and features had never been filled in. Every painting, in fact, featured some odd angle on some different body part, but none of them were completed and not one was a traditional, face-forward portrait.

"I know what you're thinking," Finn said, touching his brush to the canvas in front of him. "This guy never finishes anything."

Megan flushed. "No . . . I just . . ."

"That's what I think every time I walk in here," Finn said. "It's so bizarre. I get these inspirations and I come out here all ready to throw my vision down on the canvas, but once the rush is gone, I freeze up. It's like I don't know where to go." Finn placed his brush in a cup of water and glanced at her over his shoulder. "So, is she giving you hell?"

"Who?"

"Hailey," Finn replied.

Megan smirked. "Nothing I can't handle."

Finn turned away from his painting to smile at her. "Good," he said.

For some reason, that simple word flooded Megan with relief. Maybe it was the way he said it. Like he was proud of her. Or impressed. Or not at all surprised.

"Maybe I'll even make her repay you your Popsicle," Megan quipped.

"That's okay. I'm over Popsicles," Finn said. "I'm more of a milk shake man now." He pulled up on his belt loops and they both laughed.

Finn held Megan's gaze until she glanced away. Suddenly she was overcome by the familiar sensation of not knowing what to say next. Finn seemed like a nice enough guy, but like the rest of his brothers, he had been in on the debate about how to run Megan out of town. Was he just being nice to her because none of his brothers were around? Was it all just some kind of act?

Finn cleared his throat again and glanced at her out of the corner of his eye. Megan thought of what Evan had told her earlier that day—that the best way to deal with his brothers was to meet them head-on. Her pulse raced at the thought, but at least Finn was alone. Maybe taking them on one at a time wouldn't be as difficult. Plus, talking to Finn somehow seemed to be a lot easier than talking to anyone else in this house.

"So . . . I . . . I heard you guys talking about me last night," Megan said, looking down at her hands.

Finn's brush hand dropped and he glanced at her, clearly embarrassed. "Oh. Okay. You . . . Good."

"Good?" Megan asked.

Finn flushed. "Yeah, I do that sometimes. I was gonna say, 'You did?' but I was also gonna say, 'Not good,'" he said, putting his brush and palette down on a cluttered shelf. "I kind of have my own special language."

Megan smiled. She knew the feeling.

"So . . . you heard us," Finn said, pushing his hands into the front pockets of his jeans.

"Yeah, so . . . you all want me gone?" Megan asked.

"We were just . . . We're just kind of used to the way things were."

"I get that. I do," Megan said. "But don't you guys think that this is hard for me too? I've never had to live with this many people and my parents are gone and, well, in case you hadn't noticed, you guys are kind of . . ."

"Overwhelming?" Finn asked.

"Good word," she said.

"Look, everyone just needs an adjustment period," Finn said with a shrug. "Try not to let them get to you."

Megan looked up into Finn's gray-blue eyes and smiled slightly. "So . . . you're not one of them?"

Finn smiled in return. Like Miller, his whole face lit up and his eyes crinkled in the corners. "Having you here is . . . Let's just say it's different," he replied. "But don't worry about me. I think I can handle it."

Megan lifted her eyebrows. "Oh, you do?"

"Yeah," Finn said matter-of-factly, looking her straight in the eyes. "I do."

From: Kicker5525@yahoo.com
To: TooDamn-Funky@rockin.com
Subject: Boy Guide

Megan Meade's Guide to the McGowan Boys
Entry Five

Observation #1: Boys have no problem stealing food off your plate without asking.
I'm telling you, it's ALL ABOUT their stomachs!

Observation #2: Boys are not always on the ball.
Turns out Finn blabbers just like me sometimes.

Observation #3: Boys CAN think for themselves.
Evan sat with me at lunch and Finn totally doesn't agree with the whole "ice Megan" plan either. Maybe Doug isn't quite the evil mastermind he thinks he is.

Seven

Megan emerged from the lunch line with her tray, a rolled-up copy of *Motorcycle* magazine sticking out from the back pocket of her baggy fatigues. If she was going to be sitting outside with silent Miller again, she was bringing her own entertainment. She knew better than to hope that Evan would join her two days in a row.

"Megan! Over here!"

Aimee waved at her from the center of the cafeteria. Megan glanced at the courtyard and saw Miller already engrossed in his game. He hadn't said one word to her or Evan yesterday. As much as she was hoping to make a breakthrough with Miller, Megan decided a little social interaction might be a nice change of pace. She made a beeline for Aimee, Ria, and their friends.

"Hey," Aimee said, smiling as she dropped back into her chair.

"Hi," Megan said. "Hi, Ria."

"What's up?" Ria said. "Have you met Jenna and Pearl?" she asked, gesturing at the two girls across from her.

"No . . . hi," Megan said, sliding into the seat next to the new girls.

She recognized Pearl from the team. She had short blond hair and a round face and was busy making a bracelet from a box of colorful beads. Jenna had a long dark braid that hung down to the middle of her back and was sporting a pair of stylish aviator glasses.

"Hi," Jenna said. "You're in my Spanish class, right?"

"Sixth period with Ms. Krantz?" Megan asked. "I don't think she likes me too much."

"That's 'cuz you know more Spanish than she does," Jenna said with a grin.

"Pearl was my grandmother's name," Pearl announced, sliding a purple bead onto a thin string next to a random array of blues, greens, and aquas.

"Oh . . . okay," Megan replied. "That's really pretty," she added, gesturing at the bracelet.

"You want one? I can make you one. I make them for everybody," Pearl said excitedly. Aimee, Ria, and Jenna all raised their arms slowly. Their wrists were packed with bracelets.

"She can't sit still," Aimee explained.

"Really? I'm the same way," Megan said.

"You are?" Pearl's whole face lit up. "See? I told you guys I don't need Ritalin. Megan and I are perfectly normal. So, Megan, do you want a bracelet? I just came up with a couple new styles."

"Yeah, sure. I'd love one," Megan said.

"Great!" Pearl reached past Jenna to drop the box of beads in front of her. "Pick some colors."

Megan laughed. "Okay. Can I do it after lunch?"

"Sure! Absolutely!" Pearl replied.

"So, Megan, let's get down to it," Ria said, leaning her elbows on the table. "How, exactly, did you end up bunking in boy heaven?"

Megan took a bite of her sandwich. "I wouldn't exactly call it heaven."

"Omigod, are you kidding? The McGowan boys?" Aimee said. "They're like the hotness brigade."

Megan laughed and took a long slug of soda. "The hotness brigade?"

"What? They are!" Aimee said. "I still can't believe my sister is dating one of them."

"Please. Once those two both won best looking in eighth grade, we all knew they were gonna be swapping saliva sooner or later," Ria said, digging into her pasta.

"Ria!" her friends exclaimed.

"Ew," Aimee added, sticking her finger down her throat.

"So . . . what?" Ria said to Megan, ignoring the others. "Did you win some contest or something?"

"Our parents are old friends," Megan explained, flushed over the image of Evan and Hailey swapping spit. "My dad got transferred overseas and I didn't want to go, so the McGowans offered to let me stay with them."

"Wow. So have you, like, seen any of them naked?" Ria asked.

Jenna, Aimee, and Pearl were all rapt with attention.

"No, I have not seen any of them naked," Megan replied. She looked around and leaned in toward the table. "But I have seen most of them in their boxers."

Jenna nearly swooned. "Omigosh. Evan McGowan in his boxers. What was it like?"

Scary, Megan thought, recalling the major morning hard-on. "It was . . . interesting."

"Evan McGowan is so perfect," Pearl said. She paused in her bracelet making and looked off dreamily. "I had my first ever sexual daydream about him."

"Really?" Megan asked.

"I think most of us did," Aimee replied. "How could you not? I mean, he's such a flirt."

Megan's body heat skyrocketed and she put her sandwich down in favor of her soda. "He is?"

"What, you haven't noticed?" Ria asked. "That boy will flirt with anyone, anywhere, anytime. Even the ugly girls."

"Ria!" her friends shouted again.

Megan forced herself to breathe. *Of course he's a huge flirt,* she thought. *Did you think you were somehow special?* But even as she thought this, she realized that she had. She had thought that his comments and smiles meant something. That they *had* to mean something.

"What? It's a good thing!" Ria countered, eyes wide. "To have an Adonis like that flirting with the trolls? It's gotta be good for the self-esteem."

Okay, I'm going to smack myself right here, right now, Megan thought.

"Sorry. Ria doesn't realize that not all of us need attention from cute boys in order to have self-esteem," Jenna said, pushing her glasses up on her nose.

Megan recalled how giddy and confident she felt whenever Evan joked with her or called her Kicks and felt a wave of shame wash through her. Her feminist mother would be so appalled. *But I don't* need *his attention,* she told herself. *I just . . .* like *it.*

"Well, whatever," Aimee said. "I wish he would quit it already. He's gonna give Hailey an aneurysm and the rest of my family will suffer the consequences."

"She doesn't like it, huh?" Megan asked, swallowing hard.

"Hates it," Aimee replied, spearing some lettuce out of her salad. "She lives for that guy, I swear. To be honest, I don't see what the big deal is. He can be kind of a jerk and he isn't even the hottest one."

"Oh no. That would be Finn," Ria put in.

"Really?" Megan asked, happy for a change in subject.

"Omigod! Evan is *so* much hotter than Finn," Pearl said.

"Actually, I was talking about Miller," Aimee said.

"Miller?" they all repeated, dumbstruck.

Aimee glanced across the cafeteria at the courtyard, where Miller was leaning back in his seat, listening to his radio. "I don't know. There's just something about him," she said, narrowing her eyes wistfully as she watched him.

"Yeah, something weird," Ria said.

"Ria!" her friends scolded.

"No, I get it," Megan said. "He's like the strong, silent type."

"Yeah," Aimee said with bashful smile, sitting up straight. "Not that I could ever get a guy like that. Or any guy."

"What?" Megan asked.

"Please. Look at me," Aimee said.

"What? You're beautiful," Megan said.

"Don't even bother, Megan," Ria said, waving her fork around. "We tell this girl all the time that she's hands down the better-looking Farmer, but she refuses to believe us."

"My arms are thicker than Hailey's calves," Aimee said frowning. "Give me a break."

Ria and Jenna rolled their eyes. Aimee had broad shoulders, a lot of muscle, and maybe a little extra meat on her bones, but she was hardly a giant.

"Whatever! You guys know I'm fine with my size. Someday some guy will totally fall in love with me. Just not in high school," Aimee said. "Boys in high school are too superficial."

"Well, maybe not all boys," Megan said, glancing over at Miller, then leaning in toward the table. "Have you ever seen his smile?" she asked.

"Actually, I don't think so," Aimee replied.

"Just wait," Megan said. "It'll blow you away."

Aimee bit her bottom lip and looked out at Miller again. Suddenly he raised his fists in the air and cheered, startling the goths across the courtyard. Aimee laughed and returned to her salad.

"Well, whatever. I still say it's Finn. You guys just don't have the same refined taste as me. I like the deep, soulful type," Ria said, gazing past Megan's shoulder. "I mean, just look at the boy. Those blue eyes, that just-got-out-of-bed hair. And look at the way he dresses. Any guy that can just throw on whatever and still be that beautiful has got my vote."

Megan glanced over her shoulder and found Finn sitting at

one of the tables by the window, wearing a faded black T-shirt, baggy jeans, and his ever-present paint-splattered boots. The sun poured in through the windows on his left, highlighting his dark blond hair and his intense expression. He was surrounded by a group of guys who were all laughing and joking with each other, but Finn's concentration was riveted on the sketchbook in front of him. His hand moved quickly across the page and even when someone threw an orange past his nose, he barely looked up.

"Well, you do have to admire that level of concentration," Jenna said.

"Yeah, but it's totally pointless. That babe only has eyes for one girl," Ria said.

"Really? Who?" Megan asked.

Ria pointed with her plastic fork. "Kayla Bird."

A tall, willowy, olive-skinned beauty floated over to Finn's table in a long skirt and black boots. She lowered herself into the chair across from his and lifted her light brown, wavy hair over her slim shoulder. Finn glanced up, saw her, and instantly closed the sketchbook.

"Who's she?" Megan asked.

"Kayla Bird, junior. Artistic, beautiful, perpetually tan," Ria said.

"The girl wears string bikinis at the town pool," Aimee put in. "This is Massachusetts. I mean, who can compete with that?"

Megan stared at Kayla's back. There was a small birthmark right next to the strap of her white tank top and she was wearing a delicate, antique-looking gold watch on her slim wrist. Everything about her was graceful. Even when she lifted her water bottle to twist open the top, she looked like a ballerina.

Megan glanced over at Finn and he was looking right at her. Not at Kayla, but at her. Megan's heart skipped a beat at being caught gaping and Finn shot her a quizzical look. He waved and Megan lifted a hand to acknowledge him before quickly turning back to the table. She sank down in her seat, blushing furiously. The one McGowan boy who didn't think she was a freak and now . . . well, now he did.

"Oh! I think we know which McGowan Megan likes," Ria teased, pointing at Megan. "You're a Finn girl. I knew we'd get along."

"No, I'm not," Megan replied. "I am so not a Finn girl."

"Please. Look at your face!" Ria replied.

"She's right," Jenna said matter-of-factly. "You are blushing rather profusely."

"Well, that's just me. I do that a lot," Megan said, sitting up straight again and clearing her throat. "Trust me. I am not a Finn girl."

"Whatever you say," Ria replied, waving her fork again.

"Well, at least you're not an Evan girl, 'cuz that could be disastrous," Aimee added.

"Yeah," Megan replied, avoiding all eye contact. "At least I'm not that."

Megan headed for the locker room that afternoon, more than ready to take out the frustrations of the day on a soccer ball. Everyone in chemistry was refusing to partner with her because of her first-day mishap, and Ms. Krantz had actually scolded her for working ahead of the class level in Spanish class. Apparently she was confusing everyone around her. What was she supposed to do, forget her knowledge of Spanish verb tenses?

As she came around the corner into the physical education wing, Megan heard a couple of voices talking loudly. Someone was arguing just around the next bend, in front of the school store. And the voices sounded mighty familiar. Was that . . . Evan?

". . . know I don't mean anything by it."

"It doesn't matter if *I* know that. *They* don't know that," Hailey's voice replied. "Half the girls in school are looking at me like they know something I don't know. Do you have any idea what that feels like?"

"I don't understand. What do they know that you don't know?" Evan replied.

"They think that you like them, Evan!" Hailey replied. "They think they have something over me because you flirt with them right in front of me."

There was an exhalation of air. Megan looked behind her to see if anyone was coming, but the hallway was empty. She didn't want to be caught spying, but this was good stuff. She couldn't tear herself away.

"Hailey, that's just the way I am," Evan said. "I'm a friendly person."

"Yeah, right," Hailey said sarcastically.

"I am! And you knew that going in," Evan replied. "Come on, don't you trust me?"

"Of course I do," Hailey said. "It's just . . . well . . . imagine how you'd feel if it seemed like every guy in school wanted *me*."

Megan blinked as her heart squeezed. Hailey actually sounded kind of vulnerable there. She thought of Pearl's comment about her Evan-centered sexual fantasy. Maybe it wasn't the easiest thing, dating the hottest guy in school.

"Well, they do," Evan said lightly.

Megan rolled her eyes.

"Evan, I'm trying to be serious here!"

"Fine! Fine! What do you want me to do? Stop talking to girls entirely?" Evan asked.

"Sounds like a plan to me," Hailey replied.

Megan's jaw dropped.

"I don't believe you," Evan said.

"Neither do I," Megan said under her breath. Maybe Hailey's relationship wasn't easy, but she didn't have to try to *control* Evan.

At that moment she heard a bunch of her teammates coming down the hall. She lunged forward and yanked open the door to the locker room, pretending she had just arrived. Aimee, Ria, and a few of the other girls came around the corner, making enough noise to silence Hailey and Evan.

"Hey!" Megan said. "You guys ready to rumble?"

"You bet your ass I am," Ria said. "Can I pretend the ball is our math teacher's face? Would that be wrong?"

Megan laughed. Who knew what would happen between Evan and Hailey? She didn't care. She was finally feeling like she fit in. And if that could happen, anything was possible.

*   *   *

Megan sat on a bench in the locker room after practice while Ria worked a French braid into Megan's wet hair. Her heels bounced up and down and she glanced at her thick, black plastic watch. Her new garnet red bracelet rolled up and down her arm whenever she moved.

"How much longer is this gonna take?" she asked.

"I'm almost done," Ria replied.

Aimee walked out of the bathroom and grabbed her backpack and gym bag. "You should let it dry like that and then take it out for the party tonight," she said. "I bet your hair would look amazing all wavy."

Megan swallowed against her dry throat. "Party?" she asked, leaning forward to grab her Gatorade from between her feet.

"If you keep moving, it's only going to take longer," Ria told her.

"Fine," Megan replied. Maybe this was why she had never had a whole troop of girlfriends before. This primping stuff was just not her thing.

"Oh, yeah. The guys' soccer team is having a party tonight," Aimee told her, lifting the strap of her duffel bag over her head. "I thought I told you."

"You should come," Ria put in, leaning over her shoulder. "It's the first big party of the year and it usually ends with major drama."

"Yeah, the cops busted it up last year," Pearl said as she tied her sneakers. "It was so totally great."

"Pearl, you weren't even there," Ria said. "You were visiting your grandma."

"Well, I heard it was so totally great," Pearl replied, unfazed.

Ria grabbed a hair band from the bench and tied off Megan's braid. "There. Finished."

Megan was on her feet in an instant. "Thanks," she said, grabbing her stuff. "I guess maybe I'll see you guys tonight."

Megan turned to walk out the door just as Hailey and her friends emerged from the second row of lockers. Hailey glared at Megan. Megan rolled her eyes and pushed through the door. Hailey jumped in at the exact same second so that their over-stuffed gym bags slammed against each other and for a split second, they got wedged in.

"Rude much?" Hailey said.

Megan scrambled for a comeback, but as always, she knew she wouldn't be able to choke one out if she happened to think of one. Instead she rolled her eyes and pushed through the door.

Just once, she thought, fuming. *Just once I wish I could actually defend myself.*

"Megan! Wait up!" Aimee called out.

Megan paused just outside the door. Once again, Evan's car was parked down below. Evan stood in front of it, talking to Darnell and a couple of his friends who had just gotten out of football practice. When Megan turned around, almost the entire team had emptied out of the building.

"Here. This is Christian Todd's address," Aimee said, tearing a piece of paper out of her notebook and handing it over. "That's where the party's gonna be, but call me if you need a ride."

"You know, Aimee, I don't think Megan's going to be able to make the party," Hailey said, striding up to them. "Shouldn't you be working on your penalty kicks? We do have a game coming up."

"My penalty kicks are fine," Megan said flatly.

"Please. What were you, three for seven?" Hailey asked, glancing over her shoulder at Deena, the goalie. "It's hard to believe you really won the state championship with a leg like that. Or did you just make that up to impress all of us?"

Megan felt like she had been slapped. A few of their teammates twittered and a few others looked at one another uncomfortably.

"You know, if I were you, I'd take a look at your own skills and stop coming after me," Megan snapped. The moment the words escaped her lips, she felt a rush of adrenaline. Had she really just said that?

"My skills are just fine, thanks," Hailey shot back.

"You think so? 'Cuz I think today's practice tape would prove otherwise."

"Ooh," her teammates said under their breath.

Megan's heart hammered inside her chest. She could hardly believe what she was doing. Hailey opened her mouth to retort, but suddenly everyone was looking past Megan. She glanced over her shoulder and saw Evan walking up to them, twirling his keys around his finger.

"Hey, Kicks. We gotta go," he said, barely glancing at Hailey.

Megan flushed slightly over the triumph of the moment.

"Go where?" Hailey asked.

"We have to pick up dinner for the family," Evan said tersely.

"I can give you a ride, but you're gonna have to wait at Bamboo House."

Hailey was clearly fuming, but she managed to keep her voice under control. "Thanks anyway," she said. "Aimee, I'm coming with you."

"Oh. Okay," Aimee said. Hailey walked off and Aimee shoved her notebook back in her bag. "See you later, Megan." She glanced quickly at Evan, confused, then scurried off after her sister.

Evan stared after them stoically. Megan's heart went out to him, even though she had no idea what he was feeling. Was he disappointed that Hailey was such a jealous nut? Was he sad because they were breaking up? What?

"Let's go," he said finally, managing a tight smile. "We don't want the runts to get hungry. Trust me."

Megan folded up the address for the party and shoved it in her back pocket. She could hardly wait to get home to her computer. Megan Meade had finally, *finally* stood up for herself. Tracy was going to be so proud.

TooDamn-Funky: u told barbie off???? go Megan!!!

Kicker5525: I KNOW! I ROCK!

TooDamn-Funky: I have never been so proud.

Kicker5525: Really? Also going to a party tonight!

TooDamn-Funky: !!! mcg's have created a monster!

Kicker5525: Well I THINK Im going. . . .

TooDamn-Funky: YES YOU ARE! as ur immersion program adviser I demand it!

Kicker5525: ALL RIGHT all right I'll go.

TooDamn-Funky: and wear pink!

Kicker5525: Don't push it.

Eight

"Who're you texting?" Evan asked.

"Friend from home," Megan said, turning off her phone. She shoved it into her bag. "So . . . are you going to this party tonight?" Megan asked Evan, emboldened by the encounter with Hailey as well as Tracy's silliness.

He pulled to a stop at a four-way intersection and sighed. "Yeah, I guess. Are you?"

"I think so," Megan said, reaching back to touch her braid. "Could be fun, you know, get to know some more people."

Evan looked at her and smiled. "That's good. You should go."

"You think?" Megan asked. "You think I should go?"

"Absolutely," Evan replied. "It'll be cool."

He moved through the intersection and turned onto Oak Street. Megan fiddled with a thick string hanging from the hem of her white T-shirt. He was going to the party. He wanted her to go to the party. This was all good.

"So what was going on with you and Hailey back there?" Evan asked.

Good question, Megan thought. "Nothing," she said. "We

just had a rough practice." She glanced at him out of the corner of her eye. "Is everything okay with you guys?"

"Why? Did she say something?" Evan asked, his eyes flashing.

"No. I just . . . I guess I got that vibe," Megan replied.

"Actually, I don't really feel like talking about Hailey right now," Evan said. He pulled into the driveway and stepped on the brake. The car stopped, but Megan's heart was in overdrive. *Definitely trouble in paradise.*

"We have to tell somebody to get Finn out of the shed," Evan said as he reached around into the backseat for the food.

"I'll go!" Megan jumped out of the car.

"Great! Don't mind me. I can carry all this by myself!" Evan called after her jokingly.

Megan ignored him and jogged around the house. She was feeling so giddy her head felt light. She was starting to feel a bubble of excitement about the party. She had friends to hang out with and Evan and Hailey were on the rocks. The possibilities for the evening ahead seemed endless.

She knocked once on the door of the shed and walked in. Finn had started a new painting. A pair of slim arms were crossed at the bottom of the canvas. The outline of an angular face and a delicate neck hovered above. There was no mistaking the subject.

"Hey," Finn said, glancing over his shoulder. "What's going on?"

"Kayla Bird, huh?" Megan said, carefully sliding onto the stool.

Finn stopped painting. "How do you know Kayla?"

"I don't, but I heard all about her at lunch today," Megan said. "You like her, right?"

Finn turned his back to her and shoved both hands through his hair. When he faced her again, there was a streak of blue reaching up from his forehead and wilting one of his curls.

"I wasn't aware this was common knowledge," he said.

"Oh, please. It's so obvious," Megan replied, rolling her eyes. "Have you asked her out yet?"

"Not exactly," Finn said.

"What does that mean?" Megan asked.

"It means no," Finn said with a smirk.

"Well, there's this big party tonight. You going?" Megan asked, fiddling with her new bracelet. "Because I think you should ask her to go."

Finn stared at her for a moment and squinted. "Who are you?"

Megan laughed. "What?" she said, suddenly self-conscious. She rubbed at a kink in her neck and looked up at him through her lashes.

"No, seriously. You're all hyper and stuff," Finn said, taking a step closer to her. "Are you having an allergic reaction to something?"

"No!" Megan said. But she could see where he was coming from. She wasn't acting like herself. She was telling Finn what she really thought. She was even telling him what to do. Kind of like Tracy always did to her. Kind of like something she had never done to another person in her life. Weird.

"Look, I'm just in a good mood," Megan said, sliding off the stool. "And I guess I want to . . . spread it around or something. I'm going to the party and a bunch of people from the team are going. . . . I just think you should come too."

"And you think I should ask Kayla," Finn said.

"Why not? You never know until you try, right?" Megan said, her eyes shining. She reached out and slapped the side of Finn's arm, which was surprisingly taut. For a long moment he looked at the spot where her hand had been.

"You sure you're okay?"

Megan shrugged and shoved her hands into her pockets. "Actually, I've never felt better." She turned toward the door and paused. "Come on. We got Chinese."

"I'll be there in a sec," Finn said, pulling his cell phone out of his back pocket. He tipped it toward her and smiled. "I have a phone call to make."

Megan grinned and walked out. Tonight was going to be the first night of the rest of her life.

"Yes, Dad, I'll be careful. Don't worry," Megan said into the phone, glancing over her shoulder into the kitchen, where the entire McGowan clan was dishing out dinner. Doug was fighting with Miller over the container of spicy shrimp and Ian was beating his plate like a drum with his chopsticks.

"I know you will, Kicker," her father said. "And we're glad you're having fun and making friends. These girls sound like good people."

"They are," Megan replied with a smile.

"Are any of John's boys going with you?" her dad asked.

Megan watched as Evan served up some sweet-and-sour chicken for Caleb and felt her heart flutter. "Yeah, Evan's going to be there. And I think Finn, too."

"Good. They'll look out for you, I'm sure," he said.

"Dad—"

"Not that you need any looking out for," he backtracked. "I'm just being your father."

"I know, I know," she said, gazing at the floor. "Listen, we're about to eat, so I better go."

"Okay. Have fun," he said.

"I will. Love ya," Megan told him.

"You too," he replied.

Megan clicked off the phone and hung it on its cradle before dropping into her chair at the table. Finn passed her the fried rice and Megan took a heaping spoonful. At the end of the table, Caleb slurped up a wad of mai fun noodles and Ian stopped drumming with his chopsticks long enough to attempt to eat with them. Doug was shoveling down food with his head bent toward the plate as if he were in a dumpling-eating contest. Sean leaned back in his chair, blindly lifting forkfuls of rice to his mouth while he read from a paperback book.

"Soda, Megan?" John asked, holding out the bottle toward her glass.

"Sure," she said with a smile. She was up to about six glasses a day. This place was great.

"So, what's everyone doing tonight?" Regina asked, tucking her skirt under herself as she sat down next to her husband.

"Party," Doug said, a piece of rice dropping from his lips as he lifted his head.

"Nice. Napkin, please," Regina said. Doug rolled his eyes as

Sean handed him a napkin from across the table, never looking up from his book.

"Whose party?" John asked.

"It's Christian's," Evan said. "You know, he has it every year."

"Ah, Christian Todd's party," Regina said, spearing a piece of broccoli. "Wasn't that broken up by the police last year?"

"Yeah, but it's gonna be a lot smaller," Evan said. "He's only inviting seniors and juniors."

"Then why is Doug going?" Regina asked.

Everyone looked down the table at Doug, who paused in his shoveling. "I got connections."

Regina shook her head and glanced at Megan. "So, are you going too, Megan?" she asked.

"Yeah. Some girls from the team asked me," Megan replied. "Actually, I was going to ask you if you could possibly give me a ride. I have no idea where this place is."

"Sure. I'll drive you," Regina replied.

"Hang on. Is that really necessary?" John asked, setting down his fork. "If Doug and Evan are going, I'm sure someone can give Megan a ride."

Doug let out a sarcastic, high-pitched laugh. Evan shifted in his seat.

"Is that funny for some reason?" John asked.

Doug looked up at Megan, then at his father. "No. It's just G-Mart's driving and his car's already full up," he said. "So latah, hatah," he said, laughing again.

"Whatever that means," his father said. "Finn, are you going?"

"Oh yeah. But I kind of have a date," Finn replied, glancing at Megan with a smile.

Megan felt a rush of warmth. She had put that smile on his face. Well, her and Kayla Bird.

"You do? With whom?" Regina asked.

"Dude, did you finally snag Kayla Bird?" Evan asked.

"Yeah. Apparently," Finn said, flushing.

"It's about freakin' time, man!" Evan said gleefully. "What made you finally grow the balls to—?"

"Evan," his father said reproachfully, glancing at Megan.

"Sorry," Evan said. "Just proud of my little bro." He lifted his hand for a high five, and Finn whacked it with a grin.

"Okay, then, Evan, looks like you'll be driving Megan to and from," John said, taking a sip of his soda.

Evan stopped chewing and looked at Megan. Her stomach dropped.

"Actually, Dad, I—"

"You have a car, you'll drive her," his father said. "Is that a problem?"

The noisy table grew a lot quieter as everyone watched and waited for Evan's answer. Even Sean stopped reading, though he kept the book in front of his face. Evan wiped his palms on his jeans and swallowed.

"No. I guess not," he said finally, averting his gaze from everyone else's.

Megan's food turned into an unappetizing lump in her mouth. Why was Evan suddenly acting so weird? Hadn't he told her in the car that he wanted her to go to the party?

"Good. Now, you all remember the new curfew?" John asked, looking around the table at all of them.

"We do," Doug, Finn, Evan, and Megan droned.

"Glad to hear it," John said, taking a bite of his food. "And Evan, you're responsible for Megan. Anything happens, you get her outta there."

Interesting, Megan thought, hiding a smile. Now, by parental decree, Evan would have to hang out with her all night. Unfortunately, when she checked for his reaction to this news, Evan looked like he'd just eaten a piece of bad fish. Megan forced herself to breathe against a lump of disappointment in her throat.

"That's okay, John," she heard herself saying. "I don't need anyone to—"

"Megan, please. That's what brothers are for, right?" John said.

Megan slid a glance past Finn at Evan. He had pressed himself back in his chair and was staring at his half-full plate.

"Yeah," she said. "I guess."

But if this was the way Evan was going to act all night, she wasn't sure she wanted to be around him at all.

Tracy always said that pink was Megan's best color, but Megan was nothing if not an anti-pink girl. Still, last year for her birthday, Tracy had bought Megan a pink T-shirt that she swore worked perfectly with Megan's ankle-length forest green canvas skirt. "In case you ever want to look like a full-on girl" Tracy had said.

So when Megan took the braid out of her hair and it fanned out around her shoulders in gorgeous, never-before-conceivedof waves, she decided she was already halfway there, so why not? It was a new house, a new town, a new set of friends. Maybe it was time for a new look.

Or maybe I should have just made it a ponytail-and-sweatshirt night, Megan thought, glancing at Evan as he parked his car behind a dozen others in front of Christian Todd's tremendous stone house. She didn't feel like herself, which made it even harder to deal with Evan's coldness. When she had come downstairs to meet him, he hadn't said a thing about her hair or her outfit. He had barely said one word to her since they left the house—had hardly cast a glance in her direction. If she could rub the scuffed glove compartment and have a genie pop out of it right then and there, her only wish would be to know what Evan was thinking.

He cut the lights and for a moment there was silence. Then a few people breezed by the car, talking and laughing. Evan unhooked his seat belt and turned toward her.

"I know this is going to sound lame, but I don't think we should walk in there together," he said.

"Huh?"

"Okay, look." Evan cleared his throat. "Um, so Hailey's been kind of freaking out the past few days and it's sort of all about you."

"What?" Megan blinked in the dark. "What does that mean?"

Evan looked at the ceiling and took a deep breath. "Here's the thing. Hailey and I have been together for over a year and you'd think that would be long enough for her to, you know, trust me, but ever since you got here, she's been acting like I'm public enemy number one."

"I think that's my role, actually," Megan said, looking away.

"Anyway, she's always been kind of jealous, but with you actually living in my house? It's pretty much pushed her over the edge," Evan said.

"So . . . ?" Megan wanted to say, *Well, how is that my problem and what the hell am I supposed to do about it?* but of course she didn't.

"So I just think it would be better for everyone involved if we didn't . . . if there wasn't a scene tonight," Evan said hopefully. "Do you know what I'm saying?"

"Yeah, I get it," Megan said, trying to sound sympathetic.

She gritted her teeth and clenched her fists. Didn't he see how crazy Hailey was? How could he just give in to it?

So much for an evening of endless possibilities. The only possibility she faced now was an awkward night of flying solo.

"You're thinking what a total loser I am, huh?" Evan said, looking away, sounding sad.

Megan had to bite her lip to keep from shouting out, "Yes!" but still, it kind of touched her that he cared what she thought.

Megan shoved open the car door. "You know what? It doesn't matter," she said. "Have fun tonight."

She slammed the door and hurried up the hill to Christian's front door as fast as the small circumference of her skirt would allow. Up ahead, a few people were walking into the house, and when the door opened, the sounds of laughter and shouting voices and seriously loud music flowed out onto the lawn. Megan's heart pounded. She was suddenly filled with a wave of anxiety so strong it actually made her nauseous. But she wasn't going to let Evan see that. She swallowed hard, squared her shoulders, tossed her newly waved hair back, and walked right inside.

From: Kicker5525@yahoo.com
To: TooDamn-Funky@rockin.com
Subject: Boy Guide

Megan Meade's Guide to the McGowan Boys
Entry Six

Observation #1: Boys are moody.
Like PMS moody.

Observation #2: Boys are fickle.
Like Tracy-Dale-Franklin-at-the-MAC-counter fickle.

Observation #3: Boys are hard to read.
As if we didn't know that already.

Nine

"Omigod! Tessa! You came!"

Megan walked into the foyer and immediately a girl threw her arms around her, enveloping Megan in an entirely too tight hug. She stank of musky perfume and one of her crunchy blond curls flew directly into Megan's mouth. It tasted sour.

"I knew you'd come!" the girl shouted in Megan's ear. Half the beer in her cup slopped over the rim and hit the floor behind Megan. "So you forgive me, right? 'Cuz I swear I didn't *mean* to kiss him. I just, y'know . . . slipped!"

Megan pushed her tongue out, freeing it from the hair. A couple of guys on their way down from the second floor noticed and laughed. "Um . . . not Tessa," Megan said, awkwardly patting the girl's back.

The girl pulled away, studied Megan's face, and grimaced. "Who the hell are *you?*"

"Uh . . . sorry," Megan replied.

She slid sideways out of the foyer and headed into the room on her left, where the party was raging. Unfamiliar faces surrounded her, laughing, singing to the music, shouting to each other across the room. A group of guys checked her up and down and consulted. Apparently she scored high on their ratings scale, because one of them lifted his chin and made a move to come over and talk to her. Megan panicked and ducked out the nearest door.

In the next room four games of Jenga were being played simultaneously on a purple-felt-topped pool table. At least twenty people were gathered around, watching the action. Megan paused as a scrawny guy with clammy skin made his move. The tower teetered for a long moment, then toppled over, spraying blocks everywhere. The crowd cheered and groaned and pointed. The kid nodded and lifted a hand, then took a beer from his friend and chugged it in three gulps.

"Megan! Hey!"

Finn emerged from the crowd. His wavy hair was tousled and he was wearing a burgundy baseball T-shirt with heather gray sleeves.

"Hey. Wow." He paused and looked at her like he had never seen her before. "Your hair looks . . . wow. Wavy."

Megan laughed and felt the color rising in her cheeks. "Yes, it is that," she said.

"Nice," he said, with an admiring nod.

"Thanks."

Finn took a sip from his cup. "So, where's Evan?" he asked, looking around.

"Not a clue," Megan said. "Where's Kayla?"

"Oh, she went to the bathroom," Finn said, shouting the last word to be heard over the cheers of the Jenga crowd. "To be honest, I don't think she's having the greatest time."

"What? Why?" Megan asked.

"I'm getting the vibe that parties like this aren't really her thing," Finn replied.

"Sorry. I didn't know. I mean, when I basically twisted your arm to make you ask her here."

Finn laughed. "No, it's good. At least I finally did it. I don't know if you picked up on this, but I'm not that great with girls."

Megan smirked.

"But anyway, I think we're gonna bail early and go someplace where we can talk," Finn said, looking around as another cheer exploded from the pool table.

Suddenly an image flashed in Megan's mind of Finn taking Kayla back to the shed at his house and showing her all his unfinished paintings. The two of them, all alone in the dark night. As Megan looked up at Finn's profile, she felt a slip of something inside her chest. Whatever it was, she chose to ignore it.

"Megan! There you are!" Ria and Aimee emerged from the crowd.

"Come on! We're all dancing out back!" Aimee said, grabbing her arm. "Omigod! I knew your hair was going to look amazing like that!"

Megan laughed. "Well, I guess I'm gonna go dance," she said to Finn. "Good luck with Kayla!"

Megan followed the girls to the screened-in back porch. The wicker furniture had been pushed up against the walls. Loud hip-hop pounded from surround-sound speakers and in the middle of the slate floor, dozens of sweating kids were busting out their best none-too-impressive moves. Aimee and Ria jumped into the middle of the fray, where Jenna and Pearl were already dancing. Jenna's hair was down and she was without glasses for the first time since Megan had met her. Her arms were linked around the neck of a tall, slim guy with peach fuzz sideburns. His hands were on her butt.

"Who's that?" Megan asked.

"That's Jenna's boyfriend, Bobby," Ria replied. "They'll be making out in the woods within the next hour."

"Excuse me?" Megan asked.

"Happens every year," Aimee said. "By the end of the night it'll be like an orgy back there."

"Wow. That's . . . special," Megan said, glancing through the screen toward the backyard. She was disgusted but somehow intrigued. She tried to imagine how many people were back there. She wondered with a pang if Evan and Hailey were already among them.

It doesn't even matter anymore, Megan thought. *He's totally gutless. He threw you out of his car.* But even as she thought this, she knew that if he were to slip his arms around her right then and there, she would dance with him for the rest of the night.

Usher's latest song came on and Aimee let out such a big and excited "Wooo!" that Megan couldn't help but grin.

Enough was enough. This was Megan's first party in her new town with her new friends. It was actually her first real party ever. And for once in her life, she wanted to let go. And obsessing about Evan was only holding her back. She wasn't going to waste one more second thinking about him.

Ria, Aimee, and Pearl cheered as Megan threw up her arms and started to dance. She closed her eyes and imagined that she was back in her room in Texas dancing with Tracy to whatever was on the radio. She moved her hips, swung her hair, and let her body do its thing. When she opened her eyes again, she caught Pearl's eye and they both smiled. This was good. This felt really good.

She didn't need Evan. She didn't need a guy at all. She had come this far without one, right? Besides, all they did was mess with your brain. Who wanted that?

Bobby whispered something in Jenna's ear and she gave him a private smile. He took her hand lightly and led her off the dance floor. Jenna stumbled once but caught her balance, laughing loudly. Megan watched as they pushed through the screen door and headed out across the lawn.

"There they go," Ria said, lifting a hand.

Megan felt a stab of longing and shoved it aside. "I don't get it. I thought she was kind of . . . I don't know. . . ."

"Bookwormy and tightly wound?" Aimee asked. "Yeah, this is how she, you know, *unwinds*."

Megan was about to return her attention to the dance floor when she spotted Hailey standing next to the door. She was wearing a black tube top and a denim skirt that was so short it could have passed for a belt. She was surrounded by four guys, all of whom were practically drooling into their beers. After a long drink from her cup, she placed it on the edge of the windowsill and tossed her arms around one guy's neck. The drink toppled over and hit the floor, splattering their shoes with beer. Hailey spit out a laugh and doubled over, clinging to her man. She was beyond drunk.

Just then Evan walked in. Megan's heart took a nosedive when she saw his face. He went right over to Hailey, took her arm, and pulled her away from her circle of admirers.

Megan stopped dancing, right in the middle of all the chaos. Evan bent his head toward Hailey's and was saying something in her ear, but Hailey kept looking away. Finally a spark lit up her eyes. She turned her head toward him and yelled something right in his face. Then she stormed out the door into the backyard. Evan put his hands on his hips and took a few deep breaths. He shook his head slowly and went back into the pool room.

Megan could barely breathe.

"Hey! What's up?" Aimee asked.

"Nothing," Megan shouted.

She felt a tug in her chest. What had just happened? Was Evan okay? Did he want to leave now? Megan felt an almost physical need to go after Evan. But no, he had already made it clear that he didn't even want to be around her tonight. This was none of her business. She turned her attention back to her friends and danced.

Megan came to the top of the stairs and looked down a long hall of closed doors. A few people were milling around, some talking, some making out. A guy in a backward baseball cap came up behind her and pressed his chest into her back, squeezing her shoulder with one hand.

"Hey, hey, hey, pretty lady! You lost?"

Megan moved and crossed her arms over her chest. "Just looking for the bathroom."

"Well, then, you came to the right guy," he said. "I'm Christian Todd. You're at my party."

"Oh, hi," Megan said. "So . . . bathroom?"

"And you are . . . ?"

"Megan Meade," she replied, taking another step back as he swayed slightly.

"Oh, no way! You're the chick crashing at the McGs'! Sweet!" he said, looking her up and down. "You *are* hot!"

Megan flushed. "Uh . . . thanks. Bathroom?"

"Wow. You must really gotta go," Christian said. "It's that one right there."

He pointed unsteadily at the first door on the left and Megan slipped away from him as quickly as possible. She opened the door to the bathroom and froze. Wrong door, interesting coincidence.

In the center of the room was a double bed and lying on the bed was Evan McGowan. His feet were on the floor and his hands were curled up into fists next to his temples. He was staring at the ceiling, but he sat up straight the second the door opened.

"Hey," he said.

"Hey," she replied. "Sorry, I'll go."

"Wait," Evan said, before she could close the door. "Come in."

Megan's heart attempted to hammer its way out of her chest. Somehow she managed to close the door behind her, dropping them into relative darkness. The only light in the room came from an outdoor floodlight that was shining on the back patio.

"How long have you been up here?" Megan asked, hovering by the door.

"About half an hour, I guess," Evan said.

"I . . . uh . . . saw you and Hailey," Megan said. "Are you okay?"

Evan exhaled loudly. "No, not really. She's trying to get back at me; can you believe that? She was down there flirting with freakin' Mike Bagley and his loser friends. When I didn't even do anything."

"Well, she was a little drunk," Megan said.

Evan laughed sarcastically. "Please. She knew what she was doing when she walked in here tonight. The thing that really gets me is she's doing it on purpose. When I flirt . . . *if* I flirt . . . it's not like it's premeditated. It's just my personality. I mean, I'm a nice guy. I'm nice to girls. It's not my fault if they like me. But I've never cheated on her. Not once. You'd think that would count for something."

He flopped back again, folding his arms over his forehead. He looked so helpless. So—*dammit*—sexy.

Megan took a few tentative steps toward him and sat down on the edge of the bed. He looked down at her from under his arms and sighed again.

"I shouldn't be here with you right now for a lot of different reasons," he said.

Megan bit her lip. It was awkward talking to him over her shoulder. She pressed her hands into the mattress and turned to face his side, drawing her legs up under her. The skirt made it difficult, so she ended up sitting back on her calves. Evan moved his arms away from his face and looked at her curiously, as if he'd just noticed she was there.

"Here's what I think," Megan said, looking down at him. "Do you want to know what I think?"

Please say you want to know what I think, because I don't know if I'm ever going to be this verbal again, Megan thought.

Evan sat up and turned to face her, sitting Indian style. One of his knees touched hers.

"Hit me," Evan said.

"I think that you're a really good guy and a great boyfriend," Megan told him. "I mean, Hailey might be a little insecure, but you're always thinking about her feelings. You didn't even want to be seen with me tonight because you thought it would upset her. You really care about her. She really cares about you. Things have a way of working themselves out."

Evan stared into her eyes. Megan's heart was pounding in her ears. Her palms started to sweat and the back of her neck felt hot. Her face was inches away from Evan McGowan's. He was looking deep into her eyes. She couldn't breathe. Was she imagining it? Was he starting to lean in toward her? Could this be the moment of her first . . .

"Oh, you *have* to be kidding me!"

The door slammed back against the wall and Megan jumped. Hailey stood in the doorway, her legs spread for balance, her tube top riding dangerously low.

Evan looked from Megan to Hailey, his eyes wide. "Hailey, I know what you're thinking—"

"I come up here to talk things out with you and you're alone in the dark with her!?" Hailey shouted. "With *her*?"

"We were just—"

"Megan, don't," Evan said, causing her entire body to burn with humiliation.

"Wow. I mean, really, wow. You two are unbelievable," Hailey said, yanking up her tube top so violently she almost knocked herself over. "Have fun with your little kicker girl or whatever you call her."

"Hailey, wait!"

Evan jumped up and followed her out into the hallway. Megan raced after them and past a line of openly gaping spectators. Hailey stumbled down the stairs and disappeared into the living room just as a mass of people started up the staircase, blocking Evan and Megan's way. Evan shoved through the crowd, but it was too late. Hailey was gone. When Megan reached his side, he was standing in the foyer, struggling for breath.

"Evan—"

"That's it. I can't take this anymore," Evan said, his eyes wild. "I'm outta here."

"Evan! Wait!" Megan shouted.

But he stormed out of the house without looking back.

"No luck?" Aimee asked, pulling a lace-fringed pillow onto her lap so that Megan could sit down on the couch next to her.

"Nope," Megan said, blowing out a breath as she dropped onto the velvety cushions. She looked up at the big, bright blue fish in the aquarium next to her. He was floating right by her face, making bubbles as his mouth opened and closed. "Finn is nowhere to be found." Megan frowned and looked at her friend. "You're not mad, are you?"

"Why?" Aimee asked, propping her cheek on the back of the couch. "You didn't do anything, right? It's not your fault Hailey flipped out. And besides, that girl has spent most of her life torturing me. One night of being a little unhappy is not going to kill her."

"Thanks," Megan said. She could deal with the rest of the partygoers talking about her, but she really didn't want to lose her new friends.

The news of what had happened upstairs had spread like an oil spill and just like that, Megan had gone from unknown new girl status to "girl everyone is whispering about." She had looked everywhere for Finn to see if she could get a ride, but apparently he and Kayla had gone off for their private talk. All Megan wanted to do was go home, but she couldn't call the McGowans and ask for a pickup, because Evan would get in deep trouble for abandoning her. Aimee had been drinking and Pearl and Ria had left with some guys to go get food. Megan was stranded.

"Oh. My. God. You guys!"

Jenna zigzagged into the room from the porch and fell down on her knees in front of the couch. Her hair was a wild mess and her cardigan sweater was misbuttoned. Bobby walked in behind her and leaned back against the wall, eyes at half-mast, looking very at peace.

"Jenna? What happened?" Aimee asked.

"Okay, you are *never* going to believe who I just saw getting all naked in the woods!" Jenna said. "Hold on. Hold on. I need to be standing for this."

She pushed herself up and fell backward into some guys

walking behind her. Megan lunged to grab her, but one of the guys stood her up straight before moving on.

"Who?" Aimee asked.

"Your sister," Jenna said, pointing at Aimee. "And her boyfriend's *brother!*"

Megan felt a sudden stab of panic and sat forward.

"*What?*" Aimee demanded, looking more sober than she had all night.

"Which one?" Megan demanded.

"The 'gangsta' one," Jenna said, laughing uncontrollably as she executed some huge air quotes. "Can you believe it?"

"Doug?" Megan said, her entire throat going dry. "Hailey is out there right now having *sex* with *Doug?*"

"Scandal!" Jenna announced, waving her hands.

Megan gaped at Aimee, shocked. How could Doug do this to Evan? How could *Hailey* do this to Evan?

"This night could not possibly get any more messed up," Aimee said.

"Oh," Jenna said, holding her stomach. "Uh-oh."

Then she turned around and promptly vomited into Christian Todd's state-of-the-art aquarium.

"Oh! Nasty!"

"Jenna! Are you okay?" Aimee asked, standing up.

"Omigod," Jenna said, holding her hand over her mouth. "Omigod, I'm so embarrassed."

She turned on her heel and, shoving right by her boyfriend, stumbled for the bathroom.

"This is not good," Megan said, turning away from the

cloudy water. Between Jenna's announcement and her regurgitation, Megan was feeling a little sick herself.

"Tell me about it," Aimee said, looking after Jenna. "She's supposed to be my ride."

"I'm talking about Doug and Hailey," Megan said. She placed her hand on her stomach. "How could they do this?"

"Oh God. Don't tell me you're going to get sick too," Aimee said, sitting again.

Megan dropped her head back and breathed deeply. "No. I think I'm okay," she said. "Aside from the mental image of Doug undressing Hailey."

Aimee paled. "Great. Now *I'm* going to vomit."

"Aren't you even surprised?" Megan asked.

"Believe me, you live with my sister for sixteen years and almost nothing surprises you anymore," Aimee said.

Bobby cut through the room and stopped in front of them, his hands in his back pockets. "Uh, is either of you sober enough to drive?" he asked. "Jenna's not doing too good."

Megan sighed and glanced at her watch, then hung her head in defeat. It was already a quarter to twelve. The first test of her curfew and she was going to fail miserably. This night was definitely done and Megan was more than ready to stick a fork in it.

"I'm good," she said, shoving herself up, then reaching her hands out to help Aimee. "Let's get the heck out of here."

"It's this one, right here," Jenna directed, pointing at a small cape house that was just like all the others on the street. Megan brought the little Focus to a stop and put it in park, letting out a sigh. It was twelve on the dot.

"You sure?" Megan asked.

"Sure, I'm sure. It's my house, right?" Jenna replied. Then she narrowed her eyes and leaned forward. "They are all exactly the same, though, aren't they?"

"It's number twenty-two," Megan said, glancing at the mailbox.

"Yes!" Jenna lifted her arms. "That's it!"

Megan rolled her eyes and got out of the car. Jenna walked around to the driver's side.

"Thank you so much, Megan," Jenna said, falling against her in a hug. She still smelled vaguely of vomit. "I swear I'm never going to drink again."

"It's no problem," Megan said. She held her breath and pushed Jenna away lightly.

"Do you have a ride home?" Jenna was wobbling a little bit like she was trying not to fall.

"I'll figure something out," Megan said, looking around at the darkened street. "You just go inside. I'll be fine."

"Okay. Well, thanks again. I'll talk to you later," Jenna said.

Megan watched her walk unsteadily to the front door and waited for her to get inside. Megan took a deep breath and sat down on the back bumper of the car, pulling her cell phone out of her bag. Finn had helped her program all the McGowans' numbers in on Thursday night, in case of emergency. Who knew they would come in handy this soon?

She scrolled through her address book to Evan's name and hit the call button. On her drive through town dropping off Aimee, then Bobby, then Jenna, she had already tried him three times and had gotten his voice mail each time. And there it was again.

"Hey, it's Evan. Leave a message and maybe I'll call ya." Chuckle. Beep.

Megan groaned and hung up. If she didn't feel so sorry for Evan and if she didn't want to kiss him so badly, she knew she would be ready to kill him by now.

She sighed and scrolled to Finn's name. He was probably already home, observing the curfew like a good boy, mentally reviewing his date with Kayla. She just hoped his parents weren't hovering over him, asking questions.

Finn picked up on the first ring.

"Megan?"

"Hey, I kind of have a problem," Megan said, squinting at the street sign. "I'm stranded on Stony Brook Road. I drove a bunch of people home and now I have no ride."

"What happened to Evan?" Finn asked.

"You don't even want to know." Megan heard a girl's voice in the background. "Is that Kayla? Are you still on your date?"

"Yeah, kind of," Finn said.

"Oh God. I'm so sorry."

"Please. Don't worry about it. I'll be right there."

"I don't want to mess up your night."

"Ten minutes," Finn said. "Don't move."

He was there eight minutes later.

Megan fell into the passenger seat of Mrs. McGowan's Volvo and put her knees up on the dashboard.

"Rough night?"

"You have no idea."

"Well, it's not over yet," Finn said, looking at the clock.

"You think they're waiting up for us?" Megan asked.

"It's our first night with a curfew," Finn said, putting the car into gear. "They're probably recording our arrival times on my dad's PalmPilot."

Megan sighed and stared out the window. She wondered if Doug was home yet. Even the idea of seeing him made her ill.

"So, did you enjoy your first Baker party?" Finn asked as they approached the McGowan house. Evan's car was already in the driveway.

"It was definitely interesting," Megan replied. "How was your date?"

The front porch light flicked on just as Finn reached for his seat belt buckle. Megan's stomach dropped.

"Maybe we should save that story for another time," Finn said as his father's face appeared at the window.

"Yeah," Megan said, bracing herself for whatever was to come. "I guess we should."

From: Kicker5525@yahoo.com
To: TooDamn-Funky@rockin.com
Subject: Boy Guide

Megan Meade's Guide to the McGowan Boys
Entry Seven

Observation #1: Boys are capable of being hurt.
Even the ones that seem totally happy and confident and like
they pretty much rule the planet.

Observation #2: When the penis takes over, it TAKES OVER.
Doug slept with Hailey. He SLEPT with HAILEY. I can't even
count the number of important and obvious facts that had to
be ignored in order for this to happen.

Observation #3: Boys can be counted on.
Finn totally bailed me out when I got stranded. He even cut
his date with Kayla short to do it. Of course, when you look
at observation #2, it seems they can't ALWAYS be counted
on. So maybe there's a footnote to this one. Boys can be
counted on unless they're thinking with their penises. Of
course, Finn was on a date, so he probably was in penis-
thinking mode. Now I'm confusing myself. Hey, did you ever
notice what a funny word *penis* is? Especially when you keep
repeating it over and over . . .

Ten

Megan sat at the end of the messy breakfast table on Saturday morning, alone and on edge. All around her were used cereal bowls and half-empty orange juice glasses. She finished off her first bowl of Trix and poured herself a second one, then picked up the bowl and headed for her room. Today seemed like a good day for hiding out.

"Good morning, Megan!" Regina said brightly as she walked into the room. "Going somewhere?"

Megan paused, half out of her chair. "Actually, I was just going to bring this back to my room."

Regina picked up the coffee carafe and paused. "Oh. I hope you're not avoiding me because of what happened last night."

Megan's face burned as she recalled the scene. She and Finn sitting at this very table. John and Regina's expressions of disappointment. And those words: *You're grounded.* Words that had never been directed at Megan before. The McGowans had appreciated the fact that Megan was late because she had acted as a designated driver, but they had said they couldn't make exceptions to the rule. So Megan and Finn were off TV, video games, and social functions for one week. Luckily, Megan wasn't into TV or video games and had sworn off social functions for the immediate future. Still, the fact that she had been punished grated on her. *She had been punished.* She had never thought it was possible.

"I'm not avoiding you," Megan said finally. *I'm avoiding everyone else.* "I just have some homework to do."

"Okay, well, before you get to that, I was hoping we could talk." Regina walked over to the table with a cup of steaming coffee.

Megan glanced at the doorway, at freedom. She had been so close.

"About what?" Megan asked.

Regina looked at her, her eyes narrowed thoughtfully. "You know, you looked really nice last night. You should wear pink more often."

"Uh . . . thanks," Megan said.

"Well, anyway, I was thinking that you and I should spend some more time together," Regina said with a smile. "Just the two of us."

"Oh," Megan said. "Okay. We could do that sometime."

"Next Saturday," Regina said.

Megan blinked.

"I made appointments for us at this great little day spa downtown." Regina took a sip of her coffee. "We're going to have the works. A facial, a massage, manicures, and pedicures. I've only been once before, but it was incredibly relaxing."

The muscles in Megan's shoulders coiled into knots. Facials, massages, and manicures? That sounded like a whole lot of sitting still. Sitting still while random strangers *touched* her. The very idea of it made Megan feel stressed.

Besides, next Saturday the team had an all-day practice

session—the last one before their first game. They were supposed to elect a captain. It was beyond important.

"What do you think?" Regina asked eagerly.

"Oh . . . uh . . ." Megan looked down at her gnawed fingernails. "Actually, I think . . ."

She glanced at Regina. Her smile looked so hopeful and
excited. This woman was practically throwing herself at Megan's
feet, begging for a girly day.

Megan suddenly remembered everything the McGowans
were doing for her—how very much she owed them. And she
had already let them down twice.

"I think it sounds great," Megan said finally, forcing a smile.
Regina's grin widened.

"Perfect! This is going to be such fun!"

"Yeah," Megan replied. "Can't wait."

"You know, I have a couple of pink sweaters in my closet,"
Regina said. "You can borrow them whenever you want."

"That's okay."

"No! You should!" Regina said brightly. "Why don't we go
try them on? You can see what you think."

"Really, I—"

"Oh, stop being so polite. I insist!" Regina said, standing.
"Come on."

Slowly Megan stood up from the table and followed Regina
to the stairs. *More pink,* she thought with a sigh. *Yippee.*

"Just keep your head up, dude. Don't be afraid of the ball. You
own the ball."

Megan put her textbook aside and peeked through the blinds. In the yard down below, Ian stood with his shoulders hunched, clutching a baseball bat with his lips pressed closed in concentration. Doug stood a few yards away with a glove and a ball.

"Okay, ready?" Doug asked.

Ian nodded and Doug threw an arcing pitch right in Ian's strike zone. Ian pulled back and let her rip, line driving the ball right at Doug's head. Megan gasped.

"See?" Doug said smiling, rubbing his skull with one hand. "You're like a little Ortiz!"

Ian grinned unabashedly and Megan sat back. The guy in the backyard helping his little brother learn to hit just did not seem like the kind of guy who could sleep with his brother's girlfriend. Doug might hate Megan, but he obviously loved his brothers. Was it possible Jenna had just been mistaken about what she'd seen?

Megan sat forward on the window seat. She couldn't sit still anymore. She shut down her computer and headed outside to the shed. Finn had been in there for at least an hour. Maybe he was due for a break.

Both Ian and Doug froze when she walked out the back door.

"Hi," she said. "Nice hitting."

"Thanks," Ian replied.

"What? Nothing about the pitching?" Doug asked.

Megan shrugged and opened the door to the shed quietly. Finn was staring, his brow creased, at his half-finished painting of Kayla Bird. He had filled in a lot of the hair and had started on the neck, but the painting was still faceless.

"Hey," she said quietly.

"Hey," Finn said, glancing over his shoulder. He had the end of a paintbrush clenched between his teeth. "You're just in time."

"For what?" she asked as she slipped inside.

"My nervous breakdown," Finn said with a wry smile, dropping his paintbrush onto the easel's shelf. He pressed the heels of his hands into his eyes and sat down on an old garden bench that was pushed up against the wall. "I suck. Did you know that you are in the presence of a person who completely and utterly sucks?"

"Ouch," Megan said, wincing. She glanced at face-free Kayla. It was actually pretty freaky to look at—just the bare minimum of her facial features sketched out with pencil, surrounded by all that detail, all those colors.

"I thought after last night, you know, if I went out with her, that I would be inspired and I might actually finish this one, but . . ." Finn threw up a hand toward the painting and sighed. "I got nothing."

"So the date wasn't inspiring?"

"Apparently not," Finn said, wiping his palms on his jeans.

"So . . . what happened?" Megan asked, climbing onto the stool.

"I don't know, I just felt like . . ." Finn sat forward and rested his elbows on his thighs. "I felt like she was kind of looking down on me. She wasn't having fun at the party, fine. So we go to Starbucks and we're talking and it's like she's been all over the world, you know? And she kept asking me, have I been here, have I been there?"

"And you haven't been here or there."

"Or anywhere," Finn said, smiling wanly. "There's not a whole lot of world traveling with seven kids. It's pretty much Cape Cod and Florida."

"Right," Megan said. "Well, did you tell her that?"

"Yeah, I cracked a joke about it, but I could tell she was disappointed," Finn said. "It's like I'm some kind of leper just because I've never skied Vail or seen the Eiffel Tower."

"Oh, overrated," Megan said.

"You've seen it?" Finn asked.

"When I was a kid."

"That's right—you've been everywhere too," Finn said. Then he smirked. "Maybe you should go out with her."

"I don't think she's my type."

Finn laughed and Megan beamed.

"Well, she's definitely not a soccer party kind of girl; that much I know." His eyes dropped down and he picked at a dried paint chip on the leg of his jeans.

Megan took a deep breath. "Look, Finn, I have lived in a lot of places and I've met a lot of people and if there's one thing I've learned, it's that some people will always find a way to feel like they're better than everyone else around them," she said. "It sounds like Kayla is one of those people. She doesn't get that just because you have different experiences . . . because you like one thing and she likes another, that doesn't make her better. It just makes the two of you different." Megan bit her lip. "Did that make any sense?"

"Yeah, it did," Finn said.

"And if she thinks she's better than you, then she is just wrong," Megan said. "And not worth it."

Finn looked up at Megan and suddenly she felt totally self-conscious. But she meant everything she had said. She knew she was right. But something about the way he was looking at her was making her feel like he could see under her skin.

"Can I paint you?" Finn asked.

Megan blinked. "Okay, that's basically the last thing I ever thought you were gonna say."

Finn was on his feet and removing Kayla's painting from the easel before the rush of heat had eased from Megan's face. Suddenly he was a flurry of motion, cleaning brushes, squirting paint onto his palette, crumpling paper towels and launching them toward an overflowing trash can in the corner.

"So, can I?" he asked.

"Uh . . . I guess," Megan said, already feeling awkward.

If there was one thing Megan wasn't, it was a model. She had never seen a freckle-faced, broad-shouldered, thick-calved girl in the pages of Tracy's fashion mags. Not once.

Finn was busily arranging his easel, which faced the back wall. Megan started to push herself off her stool. "Should I—?"

"No! No. Stay right there," Finn said. He picked up his easel and turned it so that the back of the contraption was facing her and her stool. "That's good. I like the light right there."

Megan glanced up at the skylight and the blue sky beyond. "Am I gonna have to sit still for this?" she asked. "'Cuz I'm not very good at that."

Finn grinned and peeked at her over the top of his clean canvas. "Don't worry. We'll figure it out."

Megan sat and watched Finn as he worked, sketching her

outline, the pencil scraping lightly against the cloth. He was riveted, concentrating, but his arms and hands seemed to move of their own volition. Watching him was mesmerizing. Even when he looked up at her, she found that she couldn't tear her eyes away. She kept catching his glance, looking directly into his eyes. Megan's skin grew warm under his intense scrutiny. She lifted her ponytail off the back of her neck to get some air and the ends of her hair tickled her skin. Her breath came quick and shallow.

"You okay?" he asked.

Megan instantly blushed and averted her gaze. "Yeah, fine."

"'Cuz we can stop if you don't want to do this," Finn replied.

"No, I'm . . . I'm okay," Megan said. Truth be told, everything inside her and around her felt charged. She could have sat there all day.

"Good," Finn said.

Megan's whole body felt a pleasant, tingling warmth. For a split second, neither of them moved.

The sound of shouting voices obliterated the silence. Megan turned to look toward the door of the shed. The shouting was coming from inside the house and getting closer. Finally the back door creaked open and slammed and the argument went into stereo surround sound.

"Are you gonna tell me the truth? Are you gonna tell me the truth?" Evan shouted over and over again.

Finn dropped his pencil and ran out of the shed, Megan right on his heels. Doug and Evan were going toe-to-toe in the center of the yard. Evan's eyes were wild as he glared down at Doug, whose skin was blotchy and red. Their faces were millimeters away from each other. Ian had fled the scene.

"Tell me, man. Tell me what happened," Evan said, shoving Doug with both hands.

"Evan!" Finn shouted.

"You already know, man. Why you doggin' me?" Doug shouted, stepping toward him again.

"'Cuz I wanna hear you say it," Evan replied. "I want my little brother to tell me to my face that he banged my girlfriend, that's why."

"What?" Finn said under his breath.

The back door of the garage opened and Sean walked out, wiping his greasy hands on an even greasier rag. He shot Finn an inquisitive look and Finn just shrugged. Megan felt sick to her stomach. Apparently she was the only one here who knew what was going on.

"Come on, man! Come on!" Evan shoved Doug again and again until Doug was tripping backward.

"Fine!" Doug shouted, slamming Evan in the chest with both hands so that Evan had to take a few steps to steady himself. "Fine! It's true! I banged your girlfriend and when I was done, she begged for more! Is that what you wanted to hear?"

Evan screamed and launched himself at Doug, tackling him backward and slamming him into the ground. Megan shouted out as Finn and Sean raced toward the smackdown. By the time they got there, Evan had already slammed his fist into Doug's face multiple times. His knuckles were bloody. Doug's nose was a wash of red.

"Get off him, man! Get off him!" Sean shouted, trying to grab Evan's flailing arms.

"I hate you, you selfish little punk-ass loser!" Evan shouted as he pounded on Doug like a man possessed. "You make me sick!"

Finally Sean got Evan in a two-arm lock and hauled him off Doug, kicking and shouting the whole way. Finn helped his little brother sit up. The blood was everywhere. Finn ripped off his own shirt, balled it up, and held it under Doug's nose.

"What the hell happened, man?" Finn asked, catching his breath.

"Who the hell do you think you are?!" Evan shouted at Doug.

Doug pushed himself clumsily to his feet, clutching the T-shirt to his face. "You're such a hypocrite asshole," he spat at Evan.

"I'm an asshole?" Evan shouted. "You had sex with *my* girl-friend in the freakin' woods and I'm the asshole?"

"You were up in the bedroom swapping spit with new girl, playah!" Doug yelled, throwing a hand toward Megan. "Hailey threw herself at me all cryin' and shit. Whaddya want me to do?"

"What?!" Evan and Megan blurted at the same time.

"You moved on, brotha," Doug said, pointing at Evan. "Don't blame your fickle ass on me."

"Who told you that?" Evan said, shaking Sean off and advancing on Doug again. "Who said I was messing around with Megan?"

Doug's tough demeanor faltered for the first time. "Hailey. Hailey did. She said you cheated on her. You guys were done."

Evan looked at the ground. "I don't freakin' believe this," he said under his breath. "I don't freakin' *believe* this!" he shouted.

He turned and blew by Megan and Sean, heading for his car at the end of the driveway. As they all stood there, dumbfounded, they heard him peel out, heard the angry honk of a horn, and didn't move until the sound of his engine had faded into nothing.

"It's not true," Megan said finally. "Evan and I didn't hook up." She looked Doug in the eye and felt like the sadness inside her chest was going to overwhelm her. "Hailey lied to you," she said. "She lied."

Doug just stood there for a moment, breathing rapidly, looking so confused Megan almost sorry for him.

"I didn't—I didn't know . . ." Doug stammered. For a split second Megan could see the depth of the regret in his eyes. He knew he had made a mistake. A really huge mistake. He closed his eyes tightly.

"Doug, I'm sure—"

"Screw this," he said, his words muffled by the blood-soaked T-shirt. Then he turned away from them and ran into the house.

Finn let out a shaky breath and sat down on one of the lounge chairs on the patio, hanging his head.

"Are you okay?" Megan asked.

"I've just never seen them like that before," Finn said, his face slack.

"Come on. You guys must have had fights."

"Not like that," Sean put in.

Megan swallowed hard. "Really?"

"The occasional throwdown over a trashed skateboard or a lost CD, but nothing like this," Finn said.

"So this is definitely not good," Megan said.

Sean sighed. "I'd say that's a definite understatement."

*   *   *

That night Megan stared at her soccer balls, lined up on the bookcase next to her bed. She had shelved them in chronological order, from the first ball her dad had ever bought her back in Germany to the game ball from last year's semifinal match against William Clements High. In an attempt to lull herself to sleep, Megan had mentally reviewed the significance of each ball and named all of her team members from each and every team. She had gone through all fifteen balls three times. Clearly it wasn't working.

She sighed and rolled over onto her back. No matter how she tried to distract herself, there was just no stopping the endless mental movie loop of that afternoon's fight. Megan had seen plenty of fights in her time, at her old high school or on the base, but never between two people she knew. And never between two brothers.

John had gone white and speechless when he heard about the fight. He had taken Doug to the hospital to have his nose checked out. Doug was fine, but he had sat sullen and quiet through dinner. Evan was gone until sometime after dark, when he walked in without a word to anyone and went directly upstairs.

A sudden noise in the backyard sat her up straight, her heart pounding. Megan tiptoed over to the window and peered out. Someone was back there, moving around just below her window. She ducked back behind the curtain and squinted through the space between the eyelet border and the window frame until her eyes adjusted. A large cloth flicked out like a sheet and fanned out on the ground. Suddenly everything came into focus.

It was Evan. And he was laying out a sleeping bag.

Megan sat back, breathless. She glanced at her own army-issue sleeping bag, rolled up in the corner of her room. Before she could second-guess what she was about to do, she grabbed the bag and her pillow, stuffed her feet into her flip-flops, and tiptoed downstairs.

Evan looked up when he heard the door open. He was just pushing his legs into his sack.

"Hey," he said.

"Hey."

She walked over to him tentatively, clutching her sleeping bag to her chest. "I . . . saw you out here. . . ."

"My family used to do this at least once a summer, sleep out here under the stars," Evan said, directing her attention to the gorgeous night sky. "I thought this might be one of the last warm nights."

Megan nodded and hovered over him, unsure of what to do.

"So, you gonna put that down or what?" Evan asked with a small smile.

Megan laid her sleeping bag out a couple of feet away from his. She dropped her pillow near the top and shimmied inside, loving the feel of the cool cotton against her legs. Evan folded his pillow in half to prop his head up and Megan did the same.

"So, I went to Hailey's this afternoon," Evan said.

Megan's breath caught. "You did? What did she say?"

"Nothing. I never got to the door."

"Oh."

"I just don't get it. Why would she tell him that I hooked up with you?" Evan said. "Do you think it's possible that she actually *thinks* she saw us doing something?"

Megan was, for a moment, speechless. Was Evan really looking for a plausible reason to forgive Hailey for what she had done?

"I . . . I don't know," she said. "She was pretty drunk, but—"

"I know, I know," Evan said, looking at the sky again. "I mean, she told Doug we were done and I know we never had *that* conversation. She's just . . . making things up."

"Yeah. It sorta looks that way," Megan said.

Tell him she's evil. Tell him he deserves so much better, a little voice in her mind whimpered. *Tell him to just forget about her already.*

"I just don't get it," Evan said. "How could you do all this to someone you cared about? I mean, obviously she doesn't give a crap about me. That's obvious now, right?"

Megan couldn't have put it better herself, so she just stayed silent.

"You know what? I don't want to talk about this anymore," Evan said. "Let's talk about something else."

"Like what?" Megan asked.

"Like, I don't know, what do you want to do after high school?" Evan asked.

"Wow. Um . . . I . . . college, I guess?" Megan said.

"Any idea where?" Evan asked.

"I don't know," Megan said. "I think the idea of actually staying in the same place for four years is so bizarre to me that I can't fully wrap my brain around it."

"It must be hard, moving all the time," Evan said.

"You get used to it," Megan replied automatically.

"Well, I want to get the hell out of here, that's all I know," Evan said. "BC and New Hampshire are both trying to recruit me for hockey, but I'm thinking Michigan or Northwestern. Someplace that's at least a day's drive from here."

"Don't want any visitors?" Megan joked.

"At this point I wouldn't mind never seeing this family again," Evan replied.

"You don't mean that," Megan said. "It was just a . . . a bad day."

"You don't know what it's like," Evan said, gazing up at the stars. "Do you know how many times teachers have called me Sean or Finn or even Miller? Mr. Robertson has settled on calling us all 'McGowan' because he's too senile to keep us straight. It's basically impossible to have an identity in this town or to feel like I'm my own separate person. When I'm here, I'll always just be one of the McGowan boys."

Megan looked at him, shocked. "You don't really think that," she said.

"Sometimes I do," he said. His eyes grew a little wider. "I mean, don't tell anyone."

"I won't say anything," Megan said.

"I can't believe I just told you that," he said, covering his eyes with his hand. "I've never said that out loud to anyone."

Megan's heart was so full she could hardly breathe. He'd never told anyone, but he'd told her.

"It's okay, really," she assured him. "But for the record, I really don't think it's true. Everyone knows who you are."

"Yeah, well, I think Hailey just *proved* it's true," Evan said morosely, propping himself up on his elbow to face her. He ripped up a handful of grass and let it sprinkle out of his palm. "I mean, she slept with *Doug*. She's supposed to be in love with me and she slept with my little brother." He dropped back again and stared up at the sky.

Megan watched Evan's face, half in shadow, half lit by the shimmering sky above. He looked so hurt and disgusted and sad. She wanted to touch him so badly—to press her palm to his cheek and tell him that Hailey was an idiot if she didn't see how amazing he was. He was Evan McGowan. There was no way anyone could think he was interchangeable with Doug or anyone else.

Her hand inched out across the grass that separated them. Megan held her breath. She willed herself to touch him, but she couldn't. Her chest felt like it was going to explode.

"It's gonna be okay," she said finally.

Evan looked into her eyes, then down at her semi-outstretched hand. He reached over and hooked his index finger around hers.

"Thanks," he said. "I'm glad you came down here."

"Me too," Megan said.

She expected him to pull away, but he didn't. He lay down on his back and closed his eyes, his finger still crooked around hers. Ever so carefully Megan lay down on her stomach and pressed her cheek into her pillow. Before she knew it, Evan's breathing had slowed into a deep, rhythmic pattern. He was asleep, just a couple of feet away. He was asleep, and they were still touching. Megan bit her lip and grinned, gazing at their entwined fingers.

This was, without a doubt, the best night of her life.

From: Kicker5525@yahoo.com
To: TooDamn-Funky@rockin.com
Subject: Boy Guide

Megan Meade's Guide to the McGowan Boys
Entry Eight

Observation #1: Boys do tell you how they really feel.
I think you just have to be in the right place at the right time.
Or maybe be the right person.

Eleven

Sunday afternoon, Megan was so giddy she was practically bouncing in her desk chair as she surfed the web. After an hour of research on Asperger's she decided to put some of what she had learned to the test. It wasn't like she was going to be able to sit still and concentrate on homework anyway.

Megan shut down her laptop and practically skipped down the stairs. Most of the McGowan clan, Evan included, was gathered around the TV in the living room, watching a Yankee–Red Sox game. Only Doug and Miller were absent. They were all wearing battered Red Sox baseball caps, T-shirts, or jerseys, and the coffee table was loaded up with various snack bags and soda cans. Everyone in the room was riveted. Megan waited until the Yankees' manager came out to retire his pitcher before she spoke.

"Have any of you guys seen Miller?" Megan asked.

Evan glanced over his shoulder and smiled when he saw her. She grinned back.

"Basement," John answered.

"He's not allowed to watch the Yankee–Red Sox games with us," Evan explained. "Because you know, Dad would kill him."

"Ah." Megan glanced at Finn, who was sitting next to Evan, then checked on John. His eyes were trained on the TV. "Um . . . aren't you supposed to be grounded?" Megan whispered, crouching at the back of the couch.

"Shhh!" Finn said as he leaned forward for a bag of mini-pretzels. "My dad's so mesmerized he hasn't noticed me yet."

"Nice."

"So, hey, you wanna meet me out in the shed later?" Finn asked, popping a pretzel into his mouth.

"Oh, sure," Megan replied, flushing slightly.

"What're you two doing in the shed together?" Evan asked, raising his eyebrows.

Megan's flush deepened.

"An artist never discusses his work," Finn replied.

"I think it's a magician never reveals his secrets," Megan said.

"Same thing," Finn replied. Megan and Evan looked at him like he was crazy. "Okay, it's really not," he amended.

"So, you're calling yourself an artist these days?" Evan asked. "Usually you're just going off about how much you suck."

Finn punched Evan on the arm, hard. Evan punched him back. Megan rolled her eyes. "I'll see you guys later."

She headed downstairs and found Miller sitting alone on a beanbag chair in his A-Rod T-shirt and Yankees cap, watching the same game his family was watching upstairs. Megan was struck by the loneliness of it all.

"Hi, Miller," Megan said, hopping down the last couple of steps onto the floor.

There was a commercial on the TV, but he didn't look at her. "The Yankees are on."

"Yeah, I know," Megan said. "Do you mind if I watch with you?"

There was a long pause. "Okay," Miller said finally.

Megan pulled over another beanbag chair and sat down next to Miller. Another commercial was starting. It was time.

"So, I was hoping we could talk," Megan said. "I'd like to get to know you better."

Miller swallowed. "What do you mean?" He still hadn't looked at her.

"I mean, I'd like to know more stuff about you," Megan said. "I know you like the Yankees, but I don't know much else. Wouldn't you like to know more stuff about me?"

"I guess," Miller said.

"Okay, so what do you want to know?" Megan asked, leaning back in her chair.

Miller rubbed his palms on the beanbag chair, looking down at the floor. He kept rubbing faster and faster until his face started to turn red. Megan's stomach clenched, but she told herself to chill. The articles had warned her something like this might happen.

"Okay, I think I know of a way that you can ask me whatever you want to ask me," Megan said. "Miller?"

He paused, turning his blotchy face away from her slightly. "Yeah?"

"How about you tell me something about the Yankees? Anything at all. You like talking about the Yankees, right?" Megan asked.

"Yeah . . ."

"So tell me something about them and then ask me something about me right after," Megan said. "Do you want to see if you can do it?"

"I can do it."

Megan smiled. "Okay, then, go."

Miller glanced at her for a split second, then gazed at the floor again. "The Yankees were the first team ever to win four World Series in a row. Why do you smell like that?" he asked.

Megan burst out laughing and Miller looked at her uncertainly, then laughed too.

"Why do I smell like what?" Megan asked.

"Like the beach," Miller replied. "You smell like my mom at the beach."

"Coconut," she said. "I use coconut shampoo. I can't believe you can tell."

Miller smiled and nodded.

"This is good. Try it again," Megan said.

"Derek Jeter was the first captain of the Yankees since Thurman Munson," Miller said. "Are you gonna live with us forever?"

This time Miller looked up at her, right in the eye, for a good few seconds.

"Well, no," Megan said. "Hopefully for this year and maybe next year, though. Why? Do you mind me living here?"

Miller shrugged and returned his attention to the TV, which was coming back from break. "It's okay," he said, but he was smiling. "Game's back on."

*   *   *

Megan had never considered herself to be a particularly paranoid person, but as she walked into school on Monday morning, she swore she could feel different groups of girls staring at the back of her head as she walked by. When she turned to look at them, their heads were bent close together and they were whispering.

As she approached her locker, Megan quickly checked her outfit to make sure she hadn't put her cargo pants on backward. Nope, everything was normal. Maybe living with the McGowan boys was giving her some kind of anxiety syndrome. Her chest lightened slightly when she saw Pearl and Ria at Pearl's locker a few doors down from her own.

"Hey, guys," Megan said. "How was the rest of your weekend?"

Pearl's face filled up with color and she dropped to the floor to shove some books into her bag. "Fine," she said. "It was . . . fine."

"I think the real question is, how was yours?" Ria asked, holding the strap on her messenger bag with both hands.

There was something about the way she said it that made the hairs on the back of Megan's neck stand on end. Or maybe it was the pack of people that glared at her as they passed.

"Okay . . . what's going on?" Megan asked. "Did I do something?"

"You tell me," Ria said, eyeing her expectantly.

"We gotta go," Pearl said, tugging on the sleeve of Ria's sweater. "We have that homework we're gonna go over, right?"

"Yeah. See ya," Ria said dismissively.

Her face burning for a reason she couldn't explain, Megan turned to her locker and started on the combination.

"Hey," Aimee said, walking over. She looked tired as she leaned back against the wall next to Megan's locker. She let out a loud sigh and trained her eyes on the ground.

"Hey," Megan replied, taking out her history text. "Can I ask you something?"

"Sure," Aimee said.

"Is it just me or are people acting weird today?" Megan asked.

"Yeah, about that," Aimee said. "I think it's kind of gotten around that you and Evan hooked up on Friday night and that it's your fault Evan and Hailey broke up."

"What?!" Megan asked. "Who told them that?"

"I have no idea," Aimee replied, "but that's what they're all saying."

"Well, so what? It's not like it's anyone's business, right?" Megan asked.

"Look, Evan and Hailey were like the star couple around here," Aimee whispered. "Everyone looks up to them. If they think he cheated on her with you . . ."

"But he didn't," Megan said, her heart pounding. "*She's* the one who cheated on him. Evan and I are not the bad guys here."

Aimee shrugged. "Yeah, well—"

"We did not hook up, Aimee," Megan said, feeling a little bit desperate.

"Hey, I believed you on Friday and I believe you now," Aimee said as they stood up again. "It's the rest of the school you have to worry about."

"I don't care about the rest of them," Megan said, zipping up her backpack. "As long as you know the truth, I'm fine."

Aimee smiled. She gave Megan a look that was at once sympathetic and pleased. "Well, I do."

"Good," Megan said, slamming her locker door.

"It's just . . . Hailey is really not a person you want as an enemy," Aimee said as they headed off down the hall. "Trust me."

"Hi, Miller," Megan said, pushing herself away from the wall. Dozens of students streamed by her on their way into the cafeteria. They all had to dodge Miller, who stopped suddenly in the center of the doorway. "The Yankees aren't playing today, right?"

"No. It's a travel day," Miller said.

"So, I was thinking, maybe we could sit inside for lunch," Megan said, moving into the cafeteria. "It looks like it might rain, anyway."

Megan was certain that he was going to say no. He wasn't nearly ready for this yet. But then he set his jaw and nodded. "It looks like it might rain, anyway," he repeated.

Then he just started walking, chin lifted, expression almost defiant. He got to the very first table, pulled out a chair, and sat, hugging his bag in his lap. Megan followed, barely able to believe what she was seeing.

Wow, we're really making progress here, she thought, feeling proud.

She put her backpack down on the chair across from his.

"Do you want me to get your lunch?" she asked. He looked like he was barely holding it together as it was.

"Yes, please," he said, glancing up at her. "Hamburger, Coke with no ice, chocolate chip cookie."

Megan grinned. "Sounds good to me. I'll be right back. Do not move."

Miller shifted his eyes from left to right as if he were checking to make sure that no one was sitting next to him. Megan was pretty sure he wouldn't be moving unless someone picked up his chair and carried him off. She rushed through the lunch line, checking over her shoulder every so often just to make sure Miller was okay. A couple of freshman girls who normally sat at the table Miller had claimed took one look at him and then moved on to find other seats.

Back at the table, Megan placed the tray in front of Miller and let him take his food. He arranged everything the way he liked it, then looked at his meal and sighed.

"It's nice inside, right?" Megan asked.

"It's loud."

"Not as loud as you crank up your radio."

Miller smiled. Slowly he removed his backpack from his lap and placed it on the chair to his right, just as Megan had done on her side of the table. He picked up his burger and took a small bite. Soon his smile had widened into a grin.

Megan was munching on a fry, feeling giddy, when the door opened and Evan strode in. Suddenly everything inside her dropped. His jaw was clenched tightly and his eyes were narrowed into slits. He looked like a man on a mission.

Hailey's table was in the center row near the front of the room. Her friends grew hushed as Evan approached. Every soul in the cafeteria was either watching Evan to see what would happen or pointedly staring at their food in an attempt to pretend like they weren't interested. He paused next to Hailey's chair. She didn't look at him.

"Can I talk to you?" he asked.

"Sure," Hailey said, placing her bagel crust down on her plate, where all the innards had been scraped out. "Go ahead."

"Outside," Evan said.

Hailey cast a look at her friends, then pressed her hands onto the tabletop and slid from her chair. Evan stepped aside so she could lead the way out to the courtyard. As they passed her table, Megan's shoulders tensed up, but neither of them even looked at her.

Suddenly hyper-conscious of all the curious eyes around her, Megan pretended to be totally engrossed in her meal, even though she was certain that anyone within a two-table radius could probably feel the heat coming off her face.

The second the door closed behind Evan and Hailey, the room erupted in supercharged chatter. The guys at the next table threw their money down between their trays, taking odds on whether Hailey would smack Evan first or vice versa. Miller just sat there, carefully eating his lunch.

Megan tried not to stare, but she couldn't help peeking from the corner of her eye. Evan was gesticulating wildly while Hailey stood there, her arms crossed over her chest. It took a lot of self-control for Megan to keep from smiling. She knew Evan was telling Hailey that he was aware of her lie. She knew that as soon as this conversation was over, he would be free to set the record straight with his friends and the rest of the school. She knew that soon enough, Hailey and Evan would be completely and finally through.

The door was suddenly yanked open and Hailey rushed in, looking stricken and teary-eyed. She ran for the bathroom and a few of the girls at her table got up and followed. Her heart pounding, Megan looked up at Evan, expecting him to give her a nod or a smile—some sort of sign to let her know that her name had been cleared. But when she caught his eye, all the air was sucked out of the room.

Evan was looking at her like he didn't know her at all. Megan started to stand, but the second she did, Evan turned and took off across the courtyard.

Megan walked into her room that night to find Caleb bouncing up and down on her bed on all fours, meowing. Lying open on the floor was a fairly new mascara wand that had apparently been used to draw the whiskers on Caleb's face. When he saw her, he just laughed and kept bouncing. Megan was in no mood. Hailey hadn't shown up for practice. No one but Aimee and Jenna had said a word to her and she hadn't had her best game on. Now she was going to have to concentrate on three hours of homework while wondering the entire time where Evan was and what was going through his head—why he had blown her off at lunch and avoided her the rest of the day.

"Caleb! Out!" she said, holding the door open.

"Meow?" he said, pausing even though the bed continued to bounce for a second beneath him.

"Out!" she shouted.

Caleb jumped off the bed, returned to his knees, and rubbed

his head against her shin before frowning, crawling into the hallway, and closing the door behind him with his "paw." Megan cracked a smile. She grabbed her towel and robe and was just about to head for the shower when there was a knock at her door.

"Yeah?" she asked.

"It's me," Evan said.

Megan quickly checked her reflection, smoothed her hair back, and dropped her things on the bed. Her hands shook as she reached for the doorknob.

"Hi," Evan said, brushing past her into the room.

"Hi," she replied. "What's going—?"

"I just want to know why you did it," Evan said, squaring off in front of her. "Just tell me what in the hell would make you lie like that."

"What?" Megan asked, dumbfounded.

"Don't act like you don't know what I'm talking about," Evan said with a scoff. "I know what you did, Megan."

"Uh . . . okay. But I really don't," Megan said.

"Don't give me the innocent act," Evan said. "I'm not falling for it again."

"Innocent act?"

"Megan, come on. I know you told Hailey that we hooked up."

Megan felt like someone had just whacked her in the gut with a baseball bat. She lowered herself onto the edge of her bed before her knees could go out from under her.

"What?" she somehow managed to say.

"She told me. She told me how you came to her and told her you just thought she should know the truth," Evan said. "Do you even know what the word means?"

Megan looked up at him, confused. He had to be speaking another language. Nothing he was saying was making any sense.

"Evan, I have no idea what you're talking about," Megan said slowly.

"Nice try," Evan spat back. "She told me everything. How after I left, you went and found her in the solarium and told her that I'd kissed you and acted like you were just trying to be honest and take the high road or something. God! I thought you were so cool! But you're like a psycho or something. Why would you—?"

"Wait, wait, wait!" Megan said shakily, interrupting his ramble. "Just stop for a second, okay? I never did any of that."

"You never did any of that," Evan said sarcastically.

"No."

"So, what, you're telling me Hailey's just making stuff up now?" Evan asked, his eyes flashing.

Megan felt ill. He didn't believe her. "I guess so," she said.

"Are you kidding me? You're really going to stand there and deny this to my face?" Evan shouted. "Why the hell else would Hailey go off and sleep with Doug?"

"I don't know!" Megan shouted back. "But I didn't do anything."

Evan stared at her, his eyes full of hurt and confusion and denial. "I don't know what my parents were thinking, letting you stay here," he said finally. "But from now on, I want you to stay away from me."

Megan's heart tore right down the middle. "Evan, wait—"

Evan turned, walked out of the room, and slammed the door in her face.

From: Kicker5525@yahoo.com
To: TooDamn-Funky@rockin.com
Subject: Boy Guide

Megan Meade's Guide to the McGowan Boys
Entry Nine

Observation #1: Boys suck.

Twelve

Megan smoothed down the front of her navy blue T-shirt and took a deep breath to calm her nerves. She had been up half the night, but she wasn't tired. Apparently her adrenaline was doing its thing. Every time she thought about the way Evan had looked at her the night before, she wanted to throw up.

Just tell him you need to talk, Megan told herself. *What's the worst that could happen?*

But she couldn't even think about that because actually there were about a million bad things that could happen. She clenched her eyes shut in dread.

Megan grabbed her backpack and walked out into the hallway, her head held high. When she got to the kitchen, Ian and Caleb were the only ones there.

"Where is everybody?" Megan asked as they dumped their cereal bowls into the sink.

"Gone."

"What do you mean, gone?" Megan asked.

"Gone. To school," Ian said flatly. "Come on, Caleb. We're gonna miss the bus."

Caleb picked up his Spider-Man backpack and together the boys headed for the door. Megan followed them and poked her head out to check the driveway. It was empty. Megan suddenly felt hollow and exhausted.

"Okay, no big deal," Megan said, closing the door. "I'll just be a little late."

She headed out to the shed and disentangled her bike from all the others. When she placed it on the ground, it made an ugly metallic sound. Her tires were flat. The boys had declared war.

Megan sighed and trudged along the side of the garage, heading for the road. "I guess I'll just be a lot late."

"Hey!"

Megan paused at the end of the driveway. Sean was standing by the front door with a steaming mug in his hand. He was wearing a black T-shirt and jeans and his brown hair was pushed up into its usual spikes. Dark stubble covered his chin and cheeks.

"Hi," she said uncertainly.

"You walking?"

"Looks that way," Megan said.

"You're gonna be late," he replied.

"Looks that way," she repeated.

"I'll take you."

"Really?" Hadn't Sean heard about the house-wide freeze-out?

"Get your helmet," Sean said.

It was a little strange at first, straddling the bike and holding on to Sean, whom Megan had barely spoken to. But the farther they got from the house, the more Megan relaxed and enjoyed the ride. Sean had done a killer job with his bike. He was barely opening it up, but she could both hear and feel the power of the engine. He took a turn at top speed and Megan's grip on his jacket tightened slightly.

"Sorry!" Sean yelled. "Not used to passengers."

"No problem!" Megan replied. "What kind of shocks do you have?"

"Two under the rear and another up front," Sean replied after a pause.

"I can tell," Megan said. "Think you can show me your specs sometime?"

"Sure. Yeah," Sean replied.

"What year is the engine? Ninety-seven? Ninety-eight?"

"A '98," Sean replied. "But it's got a couple of new parts." He sounded confused, but Megan wasn't surprised. She knew there weren't a heck of a lot of girls out there who knew motorcycles like she did.

Sean pulled his Harley to a stop in front of Baker High. A few kids were still milling around outside, defiantly ignoring the time, while a couple more raced across the parking lot to get inside before the bell.

"Thank you so much," Megan said, lifting her helmet off as she swung her leg over the back of the bike.

"You know a lot about Harleys," Sean said.

"Yeah, well, I helped my dad restore two of them last year," Megan said. "He had to sell them both when he went to Korea, but they were really cool."

"You ride?" Sean asked.

"I have my learner's permit," Megan said, smoothing her hair back. "Well, my Texas learner's permit."

Sean nodded and for the first time since Megan had met him, it seemed like he was really looking at her. "I'll take you out for another ride sometime," he said.

"Yeah? You don't have to—"

"I'll take you out for another ride sometime," Sean repeated with an amused smirk. "You better get inside."

Megan smiled. "Well, thanks again." She started up the steps toward the school just as the other kids by the door decided it was time to head inside.

"Hey," Sean called out as he revved the engine.

Megan turned to look down at him, her helmet swinging from her fingers.

"Don't let my brothers get to you," Sean said. "They're a bunch of tools."

Megan smiled again and Sean tore off.

Miller stepped away from the wall outside the cafeteria doors when Megan approached. She couldn't have been more surprised to find him waiting for her if he had been standing there naked.

"Hi, Miller," Megan said.

"Hi," he replied, following her into the cafeteria. "Are we sitting inside again?"

Megan paused and looked out across the room. Ria, Pearl, and Jenna were already sitting at their table. All three of them had been pointedly ignoring Megan all day. Finn was at the other end of the room, sketchbook open in front of him, his back to the door. A couple of Hailey's friends stared her down from their table. Evan was nowhere to be seen.

"Why Evan McGowan would fool around with *her* I have no idea," some girl said to her friend as they walked by Megan.

"Does she even own a mirror?" the second girl replied.

"Nah, let's go outside," Megan said finally. "It's beautiful out today."

"Yeah. It's beautiful out today," Miller said with a nod. He led the way to the courtyard.

Megan and Miller dropped their stuff and went back inside to hit the lunch line. The two girls in front of Megan kept talking in low tones, then laughing obviously and loudly. She paid for her lunch and walked back outside with Miller.

"Why do you have that?" Miller asked, looking at her helmet as they sat down.

"Oh, it didn't fit in my locker," Megan said, shaking her bottled iced tea. She paused and looked at Miller, wide-eyed. "Hey! You just asked me a question."

Miller flushed and raised his shoulders, looking down at his tray. "I practiced."

"You did?" Megan asked, filling up with pride. "Miller! That's awesome!"

"What's awesome?"

Megan and Miller both looked up to find Aimee hovering next to their table with her tray. It was the first time Megan had seen her all day. Her hair was pinned back with barrettes and she was wearing a light blue shirt that made her eyes glow.

"Oh . . . nothing. Just a project we've been working on," Megan said, slightly flustered. Considering no one had talked to her or even looked at her all day, she found this a pleasant surprise. "What are you doing here?"

"I just thought it was so sunny out. . . . I thought I'd see what it was like out here," Aimee said, looking around as if she had actually never seen the courtyard before. "It's nice."

Megan's heart warmed and she and Aimee exchanged a smile. "So can I . . . ?" Aimee asked, glancing at Miller, who was very intent on arranging his tray.

"Miller, do you mind if Aimee sits with us?" Megan asked.

"Aimee?" Miller said.

"Yeah, this is my friend Aimee," Megan said.

"Hi," Aimee said.

"Hello," Miller replied without looking up.

"It's okay," Megan mouthed to Aimee.

As soon as her friend was seated, Megan reached over and arranged everything on her tray in height order. Aimee looked at it for a second, shrugged, and picked up her sandwich.

"So, how're you liking your new school?" Aimee asked Megan with a hint of sarcasm.

"Oh, I just love it!" Megan replied, playing along. "Everyone here is so *nice!*"

"Well, at least some of us are," Aimee said. "Right, Miller?"

Miller didn't respond. He clasped his hands under the table and stared at his untouched food. Aimee glanced at

Megan uncertainly. Megan put her fork down and cleared her throat.

"Hey, Miller, why don't you ask Aimee something?" Megan said. "You can use that trick we figured out the other day. You know, with the baseball?"

Miller glanced up at Megan. He had a skittish look about him, like he was a rabbit in a cage and Megan was rattling the bars. But Megan recognized the hope behind the skittishness. Miller wanted to be able to do this.

"Go ahead, ask her anything," she said. "She's really nice. I promise."

Miller's back had curved into a perfect C, but he was rigid with tension as he stared down at the table. He took a deep breath. "The New York Yankees captain Thurman Munson was killed in a plane crash in 1979," he said in a rush. "Are you in Megan's class?"

Aimee looked a little stunned but regained her composure quickly. "Uh . . . yeah," she said. "We're both juniors."

Megan grinned.

"The New York Yankees captain Derek Jeter won his first Gold Glove in 2004. Do you like baseball?" Miller asked.

Aimee laughed, glancing quizzically at Megan. Megan just shrugged one shoulder. Aimee was only going to learn who Miller was the way they all did. Slowly but surely.

"Actually, yeah," Aimee answered. "I'm an Oakland A's fan. I know, it's bizarre, but my dad grew up in northern Cal, so—"

"Did you know that Hall of Famer Reggie Jackson played for

the Oakland A's for nine years?" Miller asked, looking at Aimee for the first time.

"No . . . I didn't know that," Aimee said with a smile. "I guess you learn something new every day."

Megan smiled too. "Yeah," she said. "I guess so."

That night Megan walked out of her room just as Evan arrived at the top of the stairs. They both stopped. For a split second, Megan was certain that Evan was going to say something, but then he brushed right by her into his room. He slammed the door to his room so hard she could feel it in her bones.

She whirled around, her fingers curling into fists, and glared at his door. All she wanted to do was go over there and pound on it. Pound on it so hard it broke apart. He was supposed to be perfect.

There was a noise out back and Megan stalked to the end of the hall to look out the window. The door to the shed was just closing.

Finn.

He was just as bad as his brother. Finn had stranded her that morning too and he hadn't said a word to her about Spanish class, even though he never would have passed that pop quiz they had taken without her help. Megan turned and stormed down the hallway. Maybe she was too scared to say anything to Evan, but Finn . . . she was going to give that boy a piece of her mind.

"You guys all suck, you know that?" Megan shouted, flinging open the door to the shed.

Finn dropped his paintbrush on the leg of his jeans, where it left a streak of orange before hitting the dirty floor.

"Sorry?" he said.

"You! You suck!" Megan fumed.

"We've been over this. I know I suck."

"Not your *art*. You! You . . . *guys!*" Megan shouted.

Finn blinked. "Actually, I think I'm kind of an okay guy."

"Oh, please!" Megan said, squaring off in front of him. "I mean, what's *wrong* with you people? Were you all born like this? Because it's gotta be in your genes. Either that or you've all gotten each other in one too many choke holds over the years and you've deprived your brains of too much oxygen. Which is it?"

"Megan, I think you need to sit down," Finn said, carefully reaching for her shoulders. Keeping her at arm's length, he steered her over to the old bench and pushed her down until she had to let her knees go and fall into the seat. "Now, is this about Hailey and Evan?"

"No! It's about you! You deserted me this morning," Megan said. "And then I went to get my bike and the tires were flat. You guys popped my freaking tires! What is this? The McGowan Home for the Criminally Insane?"

"Whoa, whoa, whoa," Finn said. "First of all, I did not desert you this morning. Evan said you wanted to ride your bike to school."

"Yeah, right," Megan said.

"He did!"

"Well, I never said that," Megan replied, swallowing hard. Just the thought of Evan telling Finn that so he could avoid her made her sick to her stomach. "I guess everyone around here is a liar."

"Again, I must defend myself," Finn said, wiping his hands on an old washcloth and crossing his arms over his chest. "Have I ever lied to you?"

Megan looked up at him. "No. Not that I know of," she grumbled, averting her eyes.

"Okay, good. Now we're getting somewhere," Finn said, pulling his stool over. "Now, will you do me a favor and tell me what really happened at the party on Friday night?"

"Wow. You're kidding," Megan said. "Somebody actually wants to hear my side of the story?"

"Yeah." Finn smirked. "I do."

Megan took a deep breath and sat up straight. "Okay, I saw Hailey and Evan fighting and then Evan went into the pool room. Later I was looking for the bathroom, and I found him in this guest room, lying down on the bed. All I did was sit next to him and ask him what was up. We were just talking and the next thing I know, Hailey comes in and finds us lying there and freaks out. We went after her, but she disappeared out the back of the house. Then Evan left and that was it."

"That was it," Finn said.

"Yeah! That was it," Megan repeated. "Then like an hour later, Aimee and I are hanging out and Jenna comes in and tells us she just saw Doug and Hailey having sex in the woods. That is all I know."

"Okay, so let me get this straight. You *were* on the bed with Evan?" Finn asked.

"Big deal!" Megan rolled her eyes as she blushed. "For five seconds, I sat there."

"So Hailey didn't see anything," Finn said.

"There was nothing to see."

"And you didn't tell her that you and Evan hooked up."

"No!"

"I believe you," Finn said, standing up.

"You do?" Megan said, shocked. "You don't even want to think about it?"

"What's to think about?" Finn said, picking up the fallen brush. "You're a good, honest person who is obviously distraught about all this. Evan and Hailey totally thrive on drama. It's my expert opinion, knowing all the parties involved, that you are an innocent bystander who got sucked in by the Evan and Hailey vortex." He dipped the brush in water and swirled it around, glancing at Megan over his shoulder. "Still think I suck?"

Megan smiled. "Not so much."

"Look," Finn said with a sigh. "Evan will come around."

"You think?" Megan asked.

"Yeah, I think."

Megan wanted to believe Finn. He did, after all, know Evan a lot better than she did. But she still couldn't get that picture out of her mind—the disgusted expression on Evan's face when he told her to stay away from him. It definitely didn't seem like he was going to come around.

"Doug, however, is a little harder to call," Finn said.

Megan took deep breath. "You know what's weird? I can almost understand why Doug did it."

"Huh?"

"I mean, here's the hottest girl in school—a senior—throwing herself at you and telling you that she and her boyfriend are broken up. . . . And I know it's no excuse, but they were both really drunk. . . ."

Finn's brow knit as he laid the brush out to dry. "What are you, a guy?" he asked.

"No. Just an observer of the obvious," she replied.

"Well, look, I just want you to know that I wouldn't have left without you this morning if I had known," Finn said.

Looking into his eyes, Megan couldn't believe she'd ever thought that Finn would do such a thing. He was Finn.

"So tomorrow, we'll drive you," Finn said.

"Nah, I don't think so," Megan replied, thinking of the ice-cold shoulder she had just received from Evan. "I think I'll be taking my bike for a while."

"I thought you said someone flattened your tires," Finn replied.

"Right. I need to fix that," Megan said, pushing herself up. "Do you guys have a pump around here?"

"Somewhere," Finn said. "Probably in the garage. I'll help you find it."

"Thanks," Megan said as they walked out together. "So, any idea who I can blame this one on?"

"Too immature for Evan," Finn said, standing by while Megan picked up her bike. "I'd like to say it's too immature for Doug too, but who're we kidding? He and Ian are your best bets."

Megan sighed. "Well, at least I know who my enemies are."

"And who your friends are, I hope," Finn said.

His smile touched something inside her. She looked at the ground and wheeled her bike across the grass. "Thanks."

Megan and Finn had just reached the back door of the garage when the sound of screeching tires out on the street caught their attention. Megan leaned her bike against the wall and they walked to the end of the driveway, arriving just in time to see Doug dive headfirst into the backseat of a tricked-out Honda Civic. It had fluorescent purple running lights and rims that had probably cost more than the car itself. Megan wrinkled her nose at the smoke billowing through the windows. A couple of people cheered and shouted as the engine roared and the car peeled out. They skidded around the corner at the end of the street, completely ignoring the stop sign, and screeched out of sight.

"That can't be good," Finn said, echoing Megan's thoughts.

"Are you sure you don't want a ride, Megan?" Regina asked the next morning as she shoved her wallet and sunglasses into her purse. Megan sat at the breakfast table across from Ian and Caleb. To her right Sean was sipping coffee as he read a new book. This one was titled *City of Glass*, by Paul Auster. Megan would have to look that up on the web later.

"No thanks. I kind of like riding my bike," Megan said.

"Okay. Well, if you ever do . . ." She checked her watch and adjusted her purse strap, looking frazzled. "Doug! Let's go! I'm gonna be late for work!"

"It's printing! Keep your pants on!" Doug shouted from the rear of the house.

Regina looked at Megan. "Did he just tell me to keep my pants on?"

"I think so," Megan said with a smirk.

"That boy is lucky he did not grow up with my mother," Regina said. "He would be out of teeth by now."

"What's he doing?" Megan said.

"Spell checking his *Scarlet Letter* paper on his father's computer," Regina said. "I guess I should just be happy he's doing his homework this year, right? I had at least five parent-teacher conferences last year about him squandering his potential."

"Really?" Megan asked.

"Doug's the smart one," Sean said flatly.

"Not the only one," Regina shot back, looking at Sean pointedly as she grabbed her keys.

Sean ignored her and took a huge spoonful of Count Chocula.

"Doug!" Regina shouted.

"Patience, woman," Doug said, tromping down the hall toward them. The two black eyes left over from his fight with Evan shone in the morning light. He shoved his paper into his bag and walked right by his mother out to the front porch, where Miller was already waiting.

Regina took a deep breath. "God, grant me the serenity to accept the things I cannot change . . ." she muttered as she followed her son out. "Sean! Make sure the boys get to the bus!"

"See ya later," Megan said, getting up and placing her bowl in the sink.

"Yeah," Sean replied.

Megan grabbed her bike and pedaled off to school, thinking about the exchange between Sean and his mother. If Doug and Sean really were the "smart ones" in the family, Megan could only imagine how frustrated their parents must be. Doug spent all his time doodling and being obnoxious and Sean spent all his time playing guitar and working on his bike.

As she came around the corner at the edge of the school parking lot, Megan saw a haphazard line of people standing along the west wall of Baker High. She hit the brakes and squinted against the sun. Someone had tagged the school with blue and silver paint. She couldn't make out the design from this distance, but it took up almost the entire wall.

"What's going on?" she asked the redheaded kid who was locking up his bike across from her.

"You gotta see it," he said. "It's freakin' awesome."

Megan's brow creased as the kid took off toward the crowd and she bent to fasten the lock on her bike. A shadow fell across the sun. It was Finn and he looked nauseous.

"What?" she said.

"I told you it wouldn't be good."

Megan's heart dropped as she stood up. Every inch of her was on red alert. Her gaze trailed past him toward the school. "Oh no," she said.

"Oh yeah," he replied.

Together they hoofed it up the hill in front of the west wall and joined the throng. Teachers, students, office workers, janitors—everyone had come together to gawk, laugh, or shake their heads. Written in huge blue and silver letters were the words *Baker Sucks*. Below was an illustration, a quite good one, of a very familiar anime character peeing on a Baker High varsity jacket.

"Well, it could have been worse," one of the girls in front of Finn said. "They could have actually illustrated their point."

A bunch of people laughed and Megan and Finn exchanged a look. Megan now knew where Doug had gone the night before. And unless all the students and faculty in this place had neglected to notice Doug's self-styled wardrobe, it wouldn't be long before the rest of the school knew as well.

From: Kicker5525@yahoo.com
To: TooDamn-Funky@rockin.com
Subject: Boy Guide

Megan Meade's Guide to the McGowan Boys
Entry Ten

Observation #1: Boys have immature ways of making their points.
Like leaving you without a ride to school. Or flattening your tires. Or spray-painting really obvious graffiti involving pictures of pee.

Observation #2: Boys can chill you out with just the sound of their voices.
At least Finn can.

Thirteen

Megan had to hand it to Doug and his buddies—their inappropriate art display had definitely shifted the focus away from her and her supposed escapades. All day the graffiti was all anyone could talk about. Who had done it? Was it someone from a rival school? How had they gotten up so high on the wall? Everyone had forgotten that Megan Meade even existed.

The hallway was abuzz with the latest gossip when Megan and Finn walked out of Spanish class that afternoon. Aimee was standing across the hallway, waiting for them.

"What's up?" Megan asked.

"They're rounding up the suspects," Aimee said. "Betsy pulled Chad Linus out of my trig class right in the middle of our quiz."

"Oh, crap," Finn said, stopping in his tracks as they rounded the corner into the main hallway.

"What?" Megan said, following his gaze.

A few doors down, Doug was being ushered into one of the offices by a tall man with huge shoulders, a square jaw, and seriously thick glasses. The guy looked like Frankenstein without the neck pins.

"Who's that?" Megan asked.

"Dr. Frank," Aimee said. "The VP."

"You have to be kidding," Megan said.

"Trust me, the perfection of the name is not lost on any of us," Finn said.

Doug looked at the floor as he stepped into the office. He looked like a little kid. A little kid who was trying his hardest to appear tough but who wasn't tough at all. Her heart went out to him, but at the same time she wanted to walk over there and smack him. Had he really thought that he wasn't going to get caught?

"I'm going in there," Finn said, heading down the hall.

"What? Why?" Megan asked. "What do you think you're going to do?"

"I don't know, but he's my brother," Finn said, raising his shoulders. "Call it a sickness, but I have this stupid compulsion to help the kid."

"Okay, I get that. I do," Megan said. "But he clearly did it. Maybe he needs to get punished for it. Maybe . . . I don't know. Maybe it'll smack some sense into him or something."

Finn blew out a breath. "Megan, don't take this the wrong way, but you don't know the whole story, all right?"

"What whole story?" Megan asked.

"Doug. Why he is the way he is," Finn said. "It's not so cut-and-dried as you think. I mean, you try growing up as the twin brother of a kid like Miller. And then surrounded by five other kids. He's not a bad person, you know? He's just . . ."

Megan swallowed hard. "Your brother."

"Yeah," Finn said. "I'm not saying it's an excuse, really. It's not. I just saw what it was like for him. It's not fun when the kid next to you gets everyone's attention. And then there's nothing you can say about it because he's sick, you know?"

Megan and Aimee exchanged a look.

"Okay, but what are you going to say?" Megan asked him finally.

Finn turned and walked over to the office door. He sighed and looked up at the ceiling.

"I don't know. Maybe I'll just tell them that Doug was with me last night," Finn said.

"They'll never buy it," Aimee told him.

"She's right. You're his brother. They'll think you're just lying to get him out of trouble," Megan said, her heart starting to pound. She thought of Doug's expression after the fight with Evan the other day. She'd seen the way he was with Caleb and Ian. Somewhere under that gangsta demeanor was a good kid. Maybe he just needed someone to see it. "But they might buy it from me."

She reached for the door, but Finn grabbed her arm.

"Megan—"

"Think about it, Finn. I have no reason to protect him, right?" Megan said.

Finn considered this. "Well, you do hate his guts. So . . . why are you doing this?"

"Call it a sickness," she joked. "I don't like to see my friends suffer."

Finn smiled and Megan's heart swelled.

Megan opened the door and stepped inside, then peeked her

head back out into the hall. "You did know I was talking about *your* suffering, not his, right?"

Finn laughed. "Just go."

Megan let the door close behind her. Doug was sitting on an old pleather couch against the left wall, across from a closed door. He looked up when she walked in. On his lap was a pile of books, all of which were covered with his signature doodles. Megan clucked her tongue and grabbed the pile as she dropped down next to him.

"You know, for a supposed smart guy, you're really not that smart," Megan said, unzipping her backpack.

"What're you doing?" Doug asked.

"Saving your ass," Megan replied.

She took out a few of her own, clean notebooks and placed them in his lap, then shoved his books in her bag.

"Where's your *Scarlet Letter* paper?" she asked.

"What? You're trippin'."

"Where is it?" Megan asked again.

Doug pulled a face, leaned over, and slid the paper out of one of his notebooks. Megan placed the neatly printed pages on top of the pile of books, then zipped her bag shut.

The door opened and Dr. Frank stepped halfway out. "Who's this?" he asked when he saw Megan.

"I'm here as a witness," Megan said, standing up.

"I don't need your help, yo," Doug said, rising as well. Megan was happy to see that he had at least left his incriminating jeans at home, opting for a clean, if ripped pair.

"Yeah, right," Megan said. She held out a hand to Dr. Frank, who, after a moment of total bafflement, shook it. "I'm Megan Meade. I just started here last week," Megan said. "I have some information about Doug's whereabouts last night."

"Oh?" Dr. Frank said, crossing his long arms over his chest. "Come in, then."

Megan smiled up at the vice principal and slipped by him, followed by Doug, who, quite wisely, and for the first time since Megan had met him, kept his mouth shut. The inside of the office was like a dungeon. The walls were painted gray and there was only one dim light on the desk. The vertical blinds were pulled tight over the window and the only decorations were Dr. Frank's framed degree and a poster featuring a picture of cross-country runners with one word printed beneath it: *Discipline*.

"Have a seat," Dr. Frank said, gesturing toward the two chairs across from his metal desk.

Doug slumped into his chair. Megan sat with her back straight, perched on the edge of hers. If there was one thing she knew how to handle, it was strict adults who thought they knew everything. After growing up surrounded by army officers, a vice principal was nothing.

"Before either of you says anything, I think you should know that when we saw the anti-Baker graffiti this morning, we naturally assumed that some students from a rival school must have done the deed. But before we took the investigation to the authorities, we wanted to make sure the culprits were not walking our own halls. You can understand how embarrassing that would be."

Megan nodded. Doug shifted in his seat.

"Mr. McGowan, I have it on good authority that the . . . *character* adorning our west wall is one of your favorites," Dr. Frank said, lacing his fingers together over his stomach as he leaned back in his chair. "Most of your friends have already admitted to being involved. I'm not sure there's much you could say to exonerate him, Ms. Meade."

"Come on, man. I didn't do s—"

"Doug and I were studying together last night," Megan said, interrupting Doug before he could say something he'd regret. "I was helping him with his paper on *The Scarlet Letter*. My teacher spent an entire quarter on it last year, so I know it backwards and forwards. Anyway, we worked on it until at least midnight and Doug was already passed out by the time I left his room, so . . ."

"She was helping you with your homework?" Dr. Frank asked Doug.

"That's what she said," Doug replied belligerently.

Megan sighed. He was really not helping here.

"Can I *see* this paper?" Dr. Frank asked.

"Oh! I have it," Megan said sweetly. "I told him I'd read it over during study hall." She slid the paper out of her bag and handed it over to Dr. Frank. "It looks great, by the way," she told Doug.

Doug looked at her like she was speaking backward.

Slowly Dr. Frank flipped through the pages. Megan knew he was just stalling, trying to figure out what his next move should be.

"How do I know you're not just trying to protect Mr. McGowan?" Dr. Frank asked finally.

"Me? Protect *him?*" Megan asked. "Please. First of all, my parents are both lifers in the army and they taught me never to lie to authority figures," Megan said earnestly. *They also taught me to always be loyal to the unit, but that's beside the point.* "Second, I have no reason to protect Doug. We hate each other."

"Got that right," Doug said.

"If you hate each other, then why were you helping him with his paper?" Dr. Frank asked, looking like the cat that swallowed the canary.

"Well, I can't turn down a person who comes to me looking that pathetic and needy, now, can I?" Megan asked with an indulgent smile.

Doug rolled his eyes and looked away. For a long moment, Dr. Frank studied them both. Finally he sighed and handed the paper to Doug.

"Well, Douglas, none of your friends mentioned your involvement in the incident. I was just going on instinct here and your penchant for anime," Dr. Frank said. "Without any clear-cut evidence, I can't exactly hold you responsible."

"*See* ya." Doug noisily and dramatically pushed himself out of his chair and started for the door.

"But!" Dr. Frank called out, bringing Doug up short. "But I *can* put you and Ms. Meade here in charge of the cleanup crew."

"What? But she just *told* you I didn't do nothin'," Doug said.

"*Anything*, Mr. McGowan. And trust me, if you don't want me to look further into this matter, you will accept my generosity right now," Dr. Frank said, rising from his chair. Both Megan and Doug had to tilt their heads back to look up at him in the small space. "Get yourselves a crew and we'll have the supplies ready and waiting for you today after school."

"This is so—"

"We'll be there," Megan said, standing and opening the door. "Nice to meet you, Dr. Frank."

He smiled for the first time, exposing a line of very large, very yellow teeth. "You too, Ms. Meade."

"Hey! So what happened?"

Finn was standing right inside the cafeteria door when Megan walked in moments after her meeting with Dr. Frank. Doug had shoved her books at her, taken his own, and stormed off in the opposite direction without so much as a grunt of thanks.

"He got off . . . sort of," Megan said.

"What does that mean?" Finn asked.

"Well, he didn't get suspended."

Finn's face lit up. "Megan, that's awesome! Thank you so much."

"Yeah, well, I don't think Dr. Frank completely believed us, so we're now in charge of graffiti cleanup," Megan told him. "We have to get a crew together to meet up after school today."

"Ouch," Finn said. "Well, you've come to the right place."

They looked out across the cafeteria, where hundreds of their peers sat and ate, just waiting to be tapped for after-school labor.

"I guess I should get started," Megan said.

"What about Doug?" Finn asked.

"It's just a gut instinct, but I don't think he's going to be much help," Megan replied, walking backward. "Wish me luck."

"Good luck," Finn said with a smile.

Megan knew that most of the people in the room still had no desire to talk to her or even know her, but she didn't have a lot of options. Dr. Frank had seemed like a pretty no-nonsense guy. Who knew what her punishment might be if she failed this little task? She decided to start with her so-called friends, figuring those who had once spoken to her were the most likely to speak to her again.

"Hey, guys," she said, pushing her hands into the front pockets of her jeans as she approached the end of Ria's table.

For a moment, there was no response. Then Jenna looked up from her fruit salad quickly and said, "Hey," back.

"So . . . this is how it's going to be now?" Megan asked. "A few rumors get started and I'm suddenly contagious?"

Ria sighed and kept eating. Pearl just looked ill.

"Well, whatever, I'm not here for this. I'm here to tell you that I'm getting together a bunch of people to help clean up the graffiti this afternoon and I thought you guys might want to come."

"Shouldn't the people who did the crime do the time?" Ria asked. "Or did you do the crime?"

"I'm not a vandal," Megan said.

"Who's to say *what* you are?" Ria asked.

"Ria," Jenna said in a quiet voice.

"No, it's okay, Jenna," Megan said, her body temperature rising. "You know what, Ria? I didn't do any of those things they say I did, but that's not even the point. This isn't about me. It's about our school being defaced and whether or not you or anyone else cares enough to help out. I've only been here for a week and I can't stand it being up there. What's your excuse?"

Ria stared down at the table, looking ever so slightly smaller than she had a minute ago.

"Believe whatever you want to believe about me," Megan said. "I just hope I see you guys later."

Megan turned and headed for the next table. She didn't want to let Ria's behavior get to her, but in a way she was glad that it had. It gave her the righteous indignation she needed to face down the rest of the student body.

"Hi, I'm Megan Meade," Megan began. "I'm putting together a crew to help clean up the graffiti. . . ."

As she launched into her speech, Megan noticed that on the other side of the room, Finn was addressing a table full of artsy types. Megan caught his eye and smiled. Finn smiled back.

Over his shoulder, Megan saw Miller and Aimee sitting at their table outside. They weren't talking, but they didn't look uncomfortable either.

Megan squelched her smile and returned her focus to the task at hand. If she didn't watch out, her friends were going to kill her adrenaline rush before she ever got a chance to use it.

That afternoon, after making her excuses to a very displeased Coach Leonard, Megan headed for the west side of the school. She was just hoping that someone, *anyone* would show up. She had a feeling that even Doug's presence was iffy, and no one had paid much attention to her at lunch.

Megan came around the corner and her jaw dropped. Finn was standing in the center of a crowd of students that included

Ria, Jenna, Pearl, Aimee, and Doug, along with a few other girls from the soccer team.

"Hey," Megan said as she joined the group.

"Hi," Finn replied with a smile. "I was just explaining to everyone how this stuff works."

Open at his feet was a plastic container full of goop. There were also boxes of safety goggles, plastic gloves, and putty knives. Five ladders were lined up along the wall.

"Who put you in charge?" Megan asked.

"Well, Janitor Steve, I guess," Finn said, rubbing his hands together. "He didn't want to wait around for you to get here, so he explained the process to me. He said something about this being his bowling night; I don't know."

"Okay, so what's the deal?" Megan asked.

"We spread this poultice stuff all over the paint and it sup-posedly sucks up the color," Finn said, kneeling down and snap-ping on some plastic gloves. "Problem is it stinks and we're not supposed to get any on us."

"Great. Sounds very safe," Megan said, earning a laugh. "Let's get to work."

Everyone gathered around the boxes of protective gear and started getting outfitted. Megan found herself next to Ria and handed her a pair of gloves.

"Thanks," Ria said.

"No problem," Megan replied.

"Look, I just wanted to say I think it's really cool, you doing all of this," Ria said as she picked up a couple of pairs of goggles. "I mean, since you're new here and everything."

"Yeah, well," Megan said. "It wasn't really a volunteer thing, but I think it's important."

"It is," Ria said. She was looking at the ground as she fiddled with the strap on her goggles. Megan smiled. Humility on Ria was an odd fit, which made it all the more touching. "And, well, I'm sorry about the last couple of days. I've been kind of a jerk. I don't know why I believed Hailey anyway."

"Yeah, you do," Megan said with a laugh. "The girl is scary."

Ria laughed as well. "Yeah, but not as scary as me."

"You have a point there," Megan replied. "Come on. Let's get this over with so Coach Leonard doesn't kill us all."

Megan started to relax as she got to work. Everyone was chatting pleasantly and no one was talking about her or Evan or Hailey. With the sun pouring down on them and the sounds of the various sports being practiced in the background, Megan felt at peace.

She had just finished getting rid of the varsity jacket when Aimee came to mix the poultice.

"So, I saw you outside with Miller today," Megan said. "Did you guys talk?"

Aimee blushed. "Not really. I just like being around him."

"Yeah, that's 'cuz he ain't talkin'," Doug said, slapping some poultice onto the wall. "You'd be bored off your ass if he was."

"Ignore him," Megan said to Aimee, trying to disregard her own rush of anger. "He's just pissed at the world."

"Oh, so now you think you know me?" Doug said.

"Yeah, I do," Megan shot back. "You're smart, you're funny, you're talented, and you have an awesome family, but all you want to do is walk around like some kind of victim. It's really just annoying, actually."

Wow. Where is this all coming from? Megan wondered. It seemed like once she started voicing her thoughts, she couldn't stop herself.

Doug's skin deepened to a near purple. "You better shut your mouth, bitch, 'cuz you got no clue what you're talkin' about."

"Hey!" Finn shouted, stepping in. "What did you just call her?"

"You heard me," Doug said, his face contorted in anger.

"Apologize, Doug," Finn said.

"Yeah, right," Doug said with a scoff.

"What's your problem, man?" Finn said. "You know, Megan totally saved your ass today. You could have been suspended, *again*. You could have been expelled. You should be thanking her."

Megan crossed her arms over her chest and looked at Doug expectantly. There was a grin tugging at her lips, but she tried not to give in to it. Finn and Doug stared at each other while everyone around them waited and watched. Finally Doug broke the stalemate and looked at Megan.

"Thanks a lot," he said sarcastically. Then he yanked off his plastic gloves, tossed them at her feet, and stormed away.

Finn let out a sigh as he gazed after his brother. "You know, my parents really should have stopped with me."

Everyone cracked up laughing and they were soon back at work. Megan smiled her thanks at Finn and he picked up Doug's putty knife, brushing off the dirt and grass.

"It really was cool of you to help him out the way you did," Finn said. "Especially considering the way he's treated you."

"Well, someone told me a few things that made me rethink my position," Megan said. "I still think he needs a slap, though."

"I think you just gave him one," Finn said. "I doubt he was expecting you to tell him he was smart and funny and talented."

"I just call them like I see them."

From: Kicker5525@yahoo.com
To: TooDamn-Funky@rockin.com
Subject: Boy Guide

Megan Meade's Guide to the McGowan Boys
Entry Eleven

Observation #1: Boys are vulnerable.
Even the ones that seem like total, complete jerks.

Observation #2: Boys don't know when to call a truce already.
Especially the ones that seem like total, complete jerks.

Fourteen

Friday afternoon at lunch, Megan and Miller approached the table they had been sitting at ever since the cleanup—Aimee's usual table. They had tried it out on Wednesday. Megan didn't know how Miller would react to sitting with more than two new people for the first time ever, but he had just sat there, silently eating his lunch, and everything had been fine. Today Aimee, Ria, Pearl, and Jenna were waiting there for Megan and Miller and they already had their food. Megan could tell something was up by the way they were all sitting quietly, hands folded, trying not to smile.

"Okay . . . what?" Megan asked, almost afraid to sit down.

Miller broke into a wide grin and finally Megan saw it. Every last one of her friends' trays had been arranged just the way Miller always arranged his own. Everything was in height order from left to right.

Megan placed her tray down on the table, grinning.

"Hi, Miller," Aimee said brightly as he sat down next to her, across from Megan.

"Hello, Aimee," Miller said, blushing as he started to arrange his tray.

"Anyone sitting here?" Megan looked up to find Finn sliding into the chair next to Miller's. He was wearing a bright blue T-shirt that turned his eyes a color previously absent from nature. They were gorgeous.

"Hey," Megan said.

"Hey."

His smile reminded her of the other night, behind the house, when they had walked her bike to the garage. Megan wasn't sure why it brought that moment back, but it made her heart stir. This was interesting.

"Ladies," Finn said, nodding at the rest of the table.

"Gentleman," Ria replied teasingly.

"What's up, Miller?" Finn asked.

"That doesn't go," Miller said, looking at Finn's tray.

"Oh, sorry," Finn replied, quickly rearranging his things.

"Jeez, Finn, we're all down with the technique. What's wrong with you?" Megan joked.

"I know. I don't know what got into me," Finn said lightly. "Better?" he asked Miller.

"Yeah. This is Aimee," Miller replied, lifting a thumb in Aimee's direction. "She's my new friend."

Aimee was so surprised she actually opened her mouth into an O. "Hi," she said to Finn, though they already knew each other well.

"Hi," Finn replied. "I didn't know you had a new friend, Miller; that's great."

"Megan's my new friend too," Miller said.

Finn looked at Megan, practically beaming. "Yeah, I know. That's pretty clear."

Megan was suddenly very interested in her salad. She felt like everyone at the table was watching her and she didn't look up again until they had all started to eat. The second she did, Ria caught her eye and shot her an impressed glance.

"What?" Megan mouthed, knitting her brows.

Ria made a face and looked in Finn's direction. Everything in her expression implied that she thought Finn was here for Megan. That Finn was here because he *liked* Megan.

Megan rolled her eyes, shook her head no, and looked down at her tray again to cut Ria off from expressing anything further. Holding her breath, she cast a look toward Finn and he glanced quickly away. He had been watching her.

Megan's heart raced and she took a long sip of her soda. Ria was insane. Finn did not like her. Finn liked girls like Kayla Bird. That might not have worked out, but Kayla was clearly his type and clearly nothing like Megan. No. Ria was wrong. She just had to be.

That afternoon, after her shower, Megan decided she was going to go out back to the shed and hang with Finn. Hanging with him would be the only way to cure herself of the obsessing she had been doing all day. Ever since Ria had implied Finn liked her—an implication she had backed up with actual words at practice—Finn was all Megan could think about. Did he like her? Did she like him? What if she did like him? What then?

By the time she had brushed out her hair, she had driven herself to the brink of insanity, all because Ria had planted this seed in her head. Yesterday she hadn't been thinking about Finn at all.

Well, not really. She had to hang out with him and remind herself of what their relationship really was. They were friends. Finn didn't see her as anything more than that.

Having resolved to nip this obsession thing in the bud before it got out of hand, Megan twisted her damp hair into a braid down her back and pushed open the back door of the house. Instantly all her determination rushed right out of her. Standing in the center of the yard, deep in conversation, were two people Megan had less than zero desire to see just then—Evan and Hailey.

Megan couldn't believe it. How could these two be talking? How was it possible that he could forgive Hailey for sleeping with Doug but not forgive Megan for things she hadn't even done? They both looked up and greeted her with cold, hard stares.

"I'm going inside," Hailey said, breaking away from Evan.

Megan stared her down as she walked right toward her, but Hailey never once looked at her. Evan started after his so-called love, glaring at Megan on the way. There was so much disgust in his eyes it made her insides curl up. That was it. She couldn't take it anymore.

"Can't look me in the face, can you, Hailey?" Megan said, turning around. "Not that I blame you after all the lying."

Hailey paused at the door, but Evan whirled on Megan, his eyes flashing.

"Why don't you just leave her alone?" he said.

"You're even worse than she is, you know that?" Megan said. "At least she had a reason for what she did. I never lied to you once, but you just decided not to believe me. You're so totally snowed."

"Oh, please!" Hailey said.

"That's your big argument? 'Oh, please'?" Megan said, turning to Hailey. "Are you really going to stand there and act like we both don't know what really happened? Are you really going to lie about me to my face? You're amazing, you know that?"

Hailey glared at Megan for only a split second before she looked down at the ground.

"Ask her," Megan directed Evan. "Ask her right now if I ever found her at that party and told her that you and I hooked up. Ask her. I want to see how big of a liar she really is."

Evan stared at Megan for a long moment, clenching and unclenching his jaw.

Megan felt like a dose of bile had been injected directly into her heart. "I can't believe I ever wasted even a second of my life thinking about you."

Pushing past Hailey, Megan walked back into the house and up to her room. Her frustration was so overwhelming she felt like it was going to burst out of her veins. She grabbed her phone and dialed Tracy's number. Tracy was the only person on the planet she could talk to about this.

"Megan?" Tracy answered, surprised.

"Trace, guess what? This guy immersion program is really working," Megan said, pacing her room. She paused and looked out the window. Evan was sitting on the hammock now, head in his hands. "And you know what I'm learning?"

"Uh-oh. What?" Tracy asked.

"I'm learning that guys are totally not worth it."

*   *   *

Find a happy place, Megan. Just find a happy place . . .

Lemon, Megan's personal skin technician, slathered another layer of smelly, rank goop on Megan's face, working it into her skin with her fingertips. There seemed to be broken glass shards in the mixture. And pebbles. Whatever it was, it was grating on not only her epidermis but her last nerve.

How was this de-stressing? Megan was still tense over yesterday's confrontation with Evan and Hailey—so tense that all she had been able to think about since was getting some exercise and working it out of her system. Now she was not only being forced to sit still, but this Lemon woman was scraping her skin off.

"Relax, Megan. You're here to let yourself go," Lemon said in her airy voice, swiping her hands up to Megan's temples. Lemon's spiked hair was roughly the same color as her namesake fruit and she had a red stud in her nose that glittered every time she moved her head.

"What makes you think I'm not?"

"Well, for one, your foot has been tapping nonstop ever since you sat down," Lemon said with a bright smile. "And you haven't been able to keep your eyes closed for longer than three seconds at a time."

"So? Maybe this is me relaxed."

"Oh, sweetie. I hope not," Lemon said with a sympathetic frown. She looked down at an area of Megan's body that Megan couldn't see with her head tipped all the way back and grimaced.

"What?" Megan snapped.

"Unclench your hands, sweetie," Lemon said.

Megan loosened her fists. She hadn't even realized she was

clenching them, but the moment she let go, there was a searing pain in her palms.

"Oh. Look what you've done to yourself," Lemon said, clucking her tongue as she lifted Megan's wrist.

Megan yanked her arm away and brought both hands up in front of her eyes. There were four perfect and red half-moon marks in each of her palms, left there by her fingernails.

A symphony of cowbells played on an endless loop somewhere overhead. Megan tried to focus on the melody. Maybe if she heard it repeat five times, it would be almost time to leave.

"Now, just breathe in through your nose, out through your mouth," Lemon instructed, moving her hands up and down in front of her. "In through your nose . . . out through your mouth."

Megan did as she was told. In, out. In, out. In, out.

"Slowly, sweetie! Slowly," Lemon said. "You're not running a marathon here."

Ooh . . . running a marathon. There's *a happy place,* Megan thought.

She envisioned her feet pounding against packed dirt, her own speed blowing back her hair, the burning in her lungs as she pushed herself harder and harder. In her mind's eye, Megan saw Hailey and Evan running up ahead. She saw herself pass them. Saw the look of shock on Hailey's face. Saw Evan's admiration as it finally dawned on him how much better Megan was than Hailey. He tried to ditch Hailey and catch up with Megan, but Megan left him eating dust.

"See? You're smiling," Lemon said.

"Yeah. Are we done yet?" Megan asked.

There was no way she was ever going to exorcise the Evan and Hailey demons sitting in a plush chair with goop on her face. She needed to get to soccer practice and work out some of this energy. She had to get out of here, stat.

"Well, I'm supposed to leave it on for three more minutes, but if you feel rejuvenated, then I've done my job," Lemon said. "Do you feel rejuvenated?"

"You have no idea," Megan said.

"Okay, then. Let's rinse off," Lemon said happily.

Finally, Megan thought as she leaned her head back into the sink. *Finally this heinous spa experience is over.*

Lemon rinsed Megan with warm water and handed her a plush towel. Nothing had ever felt so good against Megan's skin. Maybe she was a little bit rejuvenated. Or maybe it was just the thought of getting outside that was making her face tingle.

"Thanks," Megan said to Lemon as she walked out of the facial room and headed back toward the locker area, where she and Regina had exchanged their clothes for spa-issue robes. She could practically feel the cleats on her freshly pedicured feet. Practice would still be going on for another hour and a half. Plenty of time for Megan to take out her aggression.

"Hi!" Regina greeted her with a psyched smile in the middle of the locker room. "All ready for our massage?"

Megan's happy train screeched to a halt. "Our what?" she asked.

"Our massage!" Regina said, standing. "The grand finale of our spa day. I booked a room for both of us."

Suddenly Megan's eyes stung with unshed tears. She had been so close to freedom.

"We're looking for Megan and Regina?" a tall, muscular man said, peeking his head into the room. He had a 1970s wave in his hair and the kind of chiseled good looks Megan only saw on the cover of romance novels.

"Right here," Regina said. "This is going to feel so good," she whispered to Megan as they followed the man out into the hall. "I bet after all that soccer playing, you could use a good rubdown."

Megan swallowed hard as the man opened the door to a smaller room. He was soon joined by another guy, practically his twin in the size department but African American and totally hot. Megan stood at the back of the small room, staring at the two tables that were draped with white sheets.

Please tell me that these guys aren't going to give us these . . . rubdowns, Megan thought, starting to hyperventilate ever so slightly.

The first guy made the introductions. "I'm Corey and this is Ben. We'll be giving your massages today."

The room was intensely hot. Still, Megan found herself clamping the neck of her robe closed as her vision blurred in front of her.

"Anyone have any problem spots you'd like to tell us about?" Ben asked.

Was it just Megan, or was he kind of giving her the eye?

"Problem spots?" she squeaked.

"You know, knots or twinges. Any spots that need special attention," Ben explained.

"Oh . . . no," Megan replied.

"I'm fine," Regina added.

"Okay, then. We'll step out while you disrobe and—"

"Dis *what?*" Megan blurted.

"Disrobe," Corey replied.

"You mean take off my *clothes?* In front of *you?*" Megan cried, holding the robe even tighter and backing up a couple of steps.

"No, we'll step out of the room for a moment," he said slowly.

"And when you come back, I'll be naked."

"You can leave your underwear and bra on if it makes you more comfortable. That's your prerogative."

"My underwear and *bra?* Are you kidding me?" Megan screeched.

"Megan, relax," Regina said, looking alarmed.

"I *am* relaxed!" Megan replied. She edged along the wall toward the door, still clutching the lapels of her robe together. "At least I would be relaxed if I was at soccer practice right now like I was supposed to be! That's how I unwind—by running and sweating and kicking the ball around. Not by disrobing and having strangers give me *rubdowns!*"

"Megan, I—"

"No, Regina, I'm really sorry, but I can't stay here," Megan rambled. "I know this is your idea of a good time and I know you really want me to be, like, the daughter you never had or whatever, but I don't wear makeup and I really don't like pink and the face wash . . . well . . . actually, I like the face wash, but this? To tell you the truth, this is my worst nightmare. I have to go."

She looked at Ben and he took a giant step away from the door.

"Thanks," Megan said.

Then she ducked her head and raced out of there as fast as her buffed and polished toes would take her.

Kicker5525: SOS!

TooDamn-Funky: where r u?

Kicker5525: public bus. not totally sure its the right 1.

TooDamn-Funky: r u running away???? don't let evan run you
away!!! unless ur coming here! then def run away!!!

Kicker5525: no. just ran out on massage with R.

TooDamn-Funky: she took u 4 massage? but u hate when
strangers touch u!!!

Kicker5525: I KNOW!!!!

TooDamn-Funky: y did you not TELL HER THAT?

Kicker5525: I think I just did. I think I just told the whole place.

TooDamn-Funky: wow when u explode u explode.

Kicker5525: beginning to sense that.

TooDamn-Funky: what now?

Kicker5525: soccer practice. then prob get grounded. again.

TooDamn-Funky: sending you good vibes.

Kicker5525: thnx. ☹ love ya!

TooDamn-Funky: u 2 my poor misguided freak girl.

Fifteen

She's going to kill me. She's going to murder me. . . .

Regina didn't seem like the killing kind, of course. If she had any violent tendencies, she would have undoubtedly hurt someone by now, living with eight men and all, but Megan couldn't stop her brain from repeating the refrain. She couldn't stop thinking about Regina's face when she'd told her she was leaving. That mixture of disappointment, shock, and anxiety—like maybe she was starting to think that she and her husband had taken in your average, everyday psycho.

"Meade! What are you doing here?" Coach Leonard asked as Megan dropped her gym bag on the bottom bleacher. "I thought you had a family thing."

"It ended early," Megan said, slightly out of breath from sprinting all the way from the bike racks.

"Well, great," Coach said. She lifted her whistle and blew. "Vargas! I'm subbing in Meade!"

Tina Vargas jogged off the field and nodded at Megan as she ran in. Megan was slightly surprised at the acknowledgment from a member of the Hailey camp, but she didn't dwell. All she could see was the ball. She had to drill that ball.

"You're here!" Aimee greeted Megan as they lined up for a throw-in. "And you look all glowy."

"Yeah, well, apparently that's what a cucumber protein pack will do for you," Megan said.

The ball came flying in and Megan jumped in front of Vithya, stopping the ball with her chest and stealing it from the opposing team. She took it upfield, dodging Jessica Peraita, who tripped herself trying to shift direction. Then two defenders charged her and she passed to Ria. Megan shoved her way around them and sprinted upfield. She was wide open in front of the net when Ria lobbed the ball back to her. Megan looked left, faking out Deena in the goal, then booted it up into the right corner. Deena ate dirt and the ball caught net. Megan's team raced in for a hug.

"That was awesome!" Aimee exclaimed.

"Where were you this morning, eating extra Wheaties?" Ria asked.

Megan smiled but didn't respond. She jogged back to the line and faced off with Hailey, more than ready to go again. As Megan expected, no matter how hard she stared at the side of Hailey's face, the girl refused to look her in the eye.

"All right, ladies! Let's see some defense out there!" Coach Leonard called.

Pearl raced out from the sidelines to drop the ball. She shot Megan a secret smile as she lifted the ball in the air. Megan cleared her throat and tried to keep a straight face. It was nice to have her friends back.

The ball dropped and Hailey got control. She dribbled upfield and Megan ran up behind her. Her blood was pumping so fast she felt like she'd drunk an entire Starbucks stockroom on her way to the field. She wasn't going to let Hailey get down-field. She just wasn't going to.

Hailey set up to pass and Megan slid to the ground, kicking her right leg out at the precise moment Hailey reached her foot back for the kick. Megan's cleat got there first and the ball careened off downfield, right to Lisa Bronson, Megan's fullback. Lisa looked almost as surprised as Hailey did, but she recovered quickly and brought the ball back. Megan clamored to her feet and raced downfield again, relishing the burning in her lungs and throat. She was feeling good. For the first time since her encounter with Evan and Hailey , she was feeling damn good.

Lisa passed to Aimee, who was instantly rushed by Kathy Cash.

"Center!" Megan shouted. "Center!"

Aimee booted the ball up and over Kathy's head, executing a perfect pass that landed right at Megan's feet. Out of the corner of her eye she could see Hailey gunning for her. Megan dribbled toward the goal and braced for impact. Hailey slammed right into her side, attempting to knock her off her feet and steal the ball. Megan grunted and shoved and struggled for control. Hailey's hand was in her face; her elbow was in her gut. Megan closed her eyes to keep from losing one to a wayward finger. She booted the ball, hip-checked Hailey away, and looked up again. The ball had trickled a few feet away into open field.

Both Ria and Jessica were running for it, but Megan was still closest. She ran for the ball and kicked it as hard as she could to Aimee, all the way across the field. Aimee stopped the ball and

Megan ran right in front of the goal. Deena's attention was on Aimee. Megan caught Deena's eye and Aimee popped the ball across to Megan. Deena reacted, but not in time. Megan jumped and headed the ball right into the center of the goal.

"Dammit!" Hailey shouted, getting right up in the goalie's face. "Deena! What the hell are you doing? Use your head!"

Deena brushed the dirt off her side and slowly turned her back to Hailey.

"We're not gonna win games without defense, people!" Hailey shouted. "She's not *that* good!"

Megan laughed and walked back upfield. She wasn't sure if anyone was paying attention to Hailey, but she didn't much care. Two goals in less than two minutes was a record for her. It felt good.

The whistle blew and Coach Leonard clapped, bringing the team to attention. "All right, let's get back to it!" she shouted. "Nice one, Meade. When you show up, you really show up!"

"Thanks, Coach," Megan replied.

"Now, come on, team, let's see if anyone can stop her!" Coach called out, blowing her whistle again. "Show me something out there!"

Megan jogged to the center of the field again and Aimee came over to wrap her arm around her shoulders.

"Let's get it on!" she said.

"You know it," Megan replied.

She lined up across from Hailey, and for the first time in days, Hailey was staring her down. Megan grinned at Hailey's determined sneer. This was going to be fun.

*   *   *

Megan sat in a circle of her teammates on the floor of the main gym. Hanging on the walls all around her were the burgundy-and-gold banners touting district, county, and state championships in all sports for the past several years. Megan stared up at the girls' soccer banner just above the caged clock. The last county championship had been won in 1996.

That's all going to change this year, Megan thought, leaning back on her elbows. She was feeling cocky and she liked it.

"All right, ladies, you know how it works," Coach Leonard said, passing out slips of paper and pencils. "First you take nominations and then you'll take an anonymous vote. I've asked Pearl to count the votes when you're done. If you have any questions, I'll be in my office."

"You don't want to stay to witness democracy in action?" Ria joked, earning a round of chuckles from the team.

"I think you girls can handle it," Coach replied. "I have some game tape to watch from last year. The new captain should come see me before she leaves. Good luck."

Coach turned and headed for the athletic offices on the other side of the gym. When the door closed, Megan looked around the circle. Everyone else was doing the same. They were all surveying each other.

"Okay, well, I guess we should do nominations," Pearl said finally.

Jessica raised her hand. "I nominate Hailey Farmer," she said before anyone could acknowledge her.

There's a big shock, Megan thought.

"Okay. Hailey, do you accept the nomination?" Pearl asked.

"Yes, I do," Hailey said gravely.

"She totally rehearsed that," Ria said in Megan's ear.

"Anyone else?" Pearl asked.

Ria sat up straight and raised her hand. Everyone looked surprised.

"Ria?" Pearl asked.

"I nominate Megan Meade."

Megan's heart slammed against her rib cage.

"*What?*" Hailey blurted. "Are you *on* something?"

Everyone started talking at once. Megan pulled her knees up under her chin, hugging her legs to her. Captain. Why would Ria nominate her for captain of a team she'd just joined? Could she do it? Did she even *want* to?

A smile crept across Megan's face.

"Hey, hey, hey!" Ria said, throwing her arms up. "Let's just vote, okay? Whatever happens, happens."

Hailey stared her down from across the circle. The air was so still Megan could hear her own heartbeat.

"Well, are there any other nominations?" Pearl asked tentatively.

The silence continued.

"Okay, then let's vote," Pearl said.

Hailey scrawled something on her slip of paper, got up, and handed it to Pearl. She walked confidently back to her place in the circle and sat down. She crossed her legs at the ankle and leaned back on her hands. One by one, everyone turned in their votes. Megan stared at her name on her own slip of paper.

Once Pearl had all the votes, she walked away from the group and tallied them up on a pad of paper. Megan couldn't watch the proceedings since Pearl was behind her, so all she could do was wait.

Finally Pearl edged her way back over to the circle. "Um . . . it's a tie."

"You have to be kidding me," Hailey said.

"No . . . it's seven votes to seven," Pearl said, looking down at her tally.

"Who voted for her?" Hailey said, pulling her legs up and leaning forward. "I'm serious. Who voted for her?"

"Uh . . . I have a name," Megan said, nonplussed.

"I'm not talking to you," Hailey snapped, shooting Megan a look. "I want to know who voted for her after what she did. You all *know* what she did. I've been on this team with you people for three years and *seven* of you voted for her?"

"I did!" Ria announced happily.

"We know *you* did," Hailey said. "What about the rest of you? Too scared to admit that you voted for a backstabbing whore for your captain?"

Megan couldn't take it anymore. Where did this girl get off?

"All right! That's it!"

Megan looked up as Aimee sprang to her feet.

"What're you doing?" Hailey asked her.

"I can't take this anymore," Aimee said, her hands shaking. "I can't sit here while you just lie like this. Megan didn't do anything, all right? She didn't fool around with Evan. She didn't even *tell* you that she fooled around with Evan. Whatever version of the story any of you have heard, it's all a lie."

Hailey's face went ashen. She looked around uncertainly before finally recovering her balance. "Aimee, sit down."

"No, I'm not gonna sit down," Aimee said, squeezing her eyes closed. Megan could tell it was taking a ton of effort for Aimee to stand up to her big sister. "I heard you, all right? I heard you telling Jessica what you did." Aimee looked around at the rest of the team. "Hailey made it all up. She was drunk and jealous and so she told Doug that Megan and Evan had hooked up when they hadn't. And then after she was done fooling around with Doug and she realized how screwed she was, she told Evan that Megan had *told* her that the two of them had hooked up so that she'd look less guilty herself. But it was all a lie. She was jealous of Megan so she blamed it all on her, when the truth is, *Megan didn't do anything.*"

The rest of the team was looking at Hailey and Aimee in shock. Megan could hardly breathe.

"She's lying," Hailey said, lifting her shoulders and laughing a bit hysterically. "She's clearly had some kind of psychotic break."

"God, Hailey, give it up already," Aimee said, turning on her sister. "I swear, sometimes I can't even believe we came from the same womb."

A few people giggled.

"She made it all up!" Hailey cried. "You guys don't believe her, do you? Jessica, tell them!"

Jessica went white and looked around the circle. "I . . . uh . . ."

A couple of other players exchanged a look.

"I don't think anyone could have made up that story, Hailey,"

Ria said. "Except maybe you," she added under her breath.

"I'm sorry I didn't say anything before this, Megan," Aimee said finally, turning to her. "I didn't know what to do."

"It's okay," Megan said with a small smile.

Whatever Hailey had done wrong, she was still Aimee's sister. Megan herself had defended Doug when she knew he had done something wrong. She could only imagine how hard it had been for Aimee to come out with the truth at all.

"I think we should re-vote," Deena said, breaking a loaded silence.

"What?" Hailey said, whirling on her. "Deena!"

But Deena just stared at Hailey. Hailey let out an indignant breath and looked around the circle. Everyone else averted their eyes. Megan watched Hailey as she realized that she was on her own. There was a panicked look in her eyes. She had just had her entire world yanked out from under her. It wasn't that long ago that Megan had experienced exactly the same sensation.

"You guys, I don't think that this should have anything to do with the captainship," Megan said.

"Huh?" Ria asked.

"This vote is about leadership of the team," Megan said. "Not who fooled around with who or who lied about it."

Everyone just stared at her for a moment.

"Okay, we're re-voting," Ria said.

"We'd have to anyway," Pearl told Megan matter-of-factly. "There was a tie."

"Yeah, because half of you people are clearly insane," Hailey snapped. But her expression didn't support her tough words. She looked pale and scared and sick.

Pearl walked around the circle and handed out new slips of paper. Slowly everyone wrote down their choice. Megan's heart skipped around in her chest. She had no idea what to hope for.

Once again Hailey was the first to hand her vote in, and this time she stayed on her feet as Pearl counted the votes. It took half the time it had before. Megan held her breath.

"The final count is three for Hailey, eleven for Megan," Pearl said. "Megan Meade is our new captain."

Megan skidded to a stop right in front of the shed. She pushed open the door of Finn's little studio, grinning like a madwoman.

"Hey! What's going on?" Finn asked, smiling.

"I got captain! I won captain!" Megan said breathlessly. She still couldn't seem to wrap her brain around it herself.

"What? You're kidding!" Finn said, his whole face lighting up. "That's awesome!"

"Oh my God, it was so cool!" Megan said, walking over and pulling him down on the bench by his sleeve. "First we voted, and there was a tie. And then Hailey freaks out saying I'm like this huge liar, so then *Aimee* gets up and she tells everybody that *Hailey's* the liar."

"Wow. Seriously?" Finn asked.

"Yeah! It was this whole huge deal," Megan said. "But then we re-voted and I won! I still can't believe it."

"Well, congratulations," Finn said.

"Thanks. I couldn't wait to tell you," Megan said, grinning at him. "You should have seen her face. It was like . . ."

Megan stopped suddenly—Finn's face had gone all weird. He wasn't smiling anymore. It seemed like he had stopped breathing.

"What?" Megan said, her heart skipping a beat. He was studying her. Taking in every line of her face from her jaw to her cheekbone to her flyaway hair.

Finn reached over and ran his hand quickly over her hair, brushing it back. "This," he said.

And then he leaned forward and kissed her. For an infinitesimal moment, Megan froze. She had no idea what to do with herself. No idea where to put her hands or whether to move her lips or how to even breathe.

Kiss him back, for God's sake! she told herself.

Then she stifled a surprised, embarrassed, happy laugh and did as she was told. She returned his pressure and reached up to grab awkwardly at his sleeve. Finn's hand cupped the back of her head and his other hand lightly touched her knee. Megan's skin was on fire. Finn was kissing her. *Finn* was kissing her!

He pulled back, out of nowhere, and looked her in the eyes. "Is this okay?" he asked.

Megan mutely, dumbly, breathlessly nodded. She just wanted his lips on hers. He smiled and kissed her again, and this time Megan slid forward on the bench, leaning her body closer to his. What she couldn't believe was how perfect this felt. How excited and happy and thrilling and safe all at the same time.

And then it hit her: Finn was the one.

The one she'd wanted to share her great news with. The one she could talk to. The one she always thought of when something funny or weird or interesting happened. Finn was smart and hilarious and kind and thoughtful.

Why did I waste my time thinking about Evan? Megan wondered as Finn lightly trailed a finger down her cheek. *How could I have done that when Finn was right here all along?*

All she wanted to do was get as close to him as possible. It was suddenly impossible to believe that she had lasted this long in life without feeling this way.

The door behind Megan let out its telltale squeak and Finn sprang away from her so fast she almost fell forward. It wasn't fast enough, however. Regina stood in the doorway, her arms crossed tightly over her stomach.

Megan gulped in a breath and looked at Finn, who hung his head as low as it could go. Yes, Finn McGowan was a lot of great things. But now he was also a dead man.

From: Kicker5525@yahoo.com
To: TooDamn-Funky@rockin.com
Subject: OMG OMG OMG

I KISSED FINN! I KISSED FINN! OMG I KISSED FINN. WHERE ARE
YOU!!!???

Sixteen

Megan sat up straight on a chair in the kitchen, hovering some-where between ecstasy and dread. Regina and John were in the next room, talking in low tones, trying to figure out what to do with her. Megan knew she should be working out a reason for them not to throw her out of their house, but she couldn't stop thinking about Finn. And every time she did, she shivered happily.

She still felt the sweep of Finn's fingertip on her cheek. His hand running over her hair. Her lips were still tingly from Finn's kiss. The way he had looked at her made her feel so beautiful. She actually felt beautiful and . . . noticed.

Regina and John walked into the room and Megan sat up even taller. She wondered if they could see her lips throbbing. Regina was clearly exhausted and John's face was creased with concern.

"Well, I'll be honest with you, Megan. We don't know what to do here," John said finally, rubbing the back of his neck. "You knew the rules and we had hoped that last week's grounding would have resonated with you somehow, but obviously it hasn't. So what do we do?"

Megan eyed him uncertainly.

Finn walked into the room behind his parents and Megan's entire being lit up. Both Regina and John glanced around.

"Hey. I know you guys told me to wait in my room, but I have something to say," Finn said, rubbing his hands on his jeans.

"Okay," Regina said. She almost looked hopeful, like Finn might have come up with an explanation to erase what she had seen.

Finn cleared his throat. "It wasn't Megan's fault. She shouldn't be punished, because it was me. It was all me. I kissed her, so you should really just do whatever you're going to do . . . to me."

"Nice try, kiddo, but it takes two to tango," John said.

"Yeah, I know, technically," Finn said. "But I mean, Megan didn't even kiss me back . . . right?"

As Finn spoke, his face grew red from the neck up. He looked at Megan, his eyebrows raised, waiting for her to corroborate his story. Megan couldn't believe what she was hearing. Had she actually done it so wrong that Finn really didn't think she had reciprocated? Or was he just being the coolest guy ever and trying to save her butt?

"Right," she said finally. "It kinda came out of nowhere. . . ."

Megan didn't know what else to say, so she shut her mouth. Regina and John looked at each other, communicating silently. Finally John blew out a sigh. Megan couldn't help but notice that they both looked relieved.

"All right, then. Finn, you knew the rules as well and you ignored them, so you're grounded. Again," his father said. "You'll go to school and you'll do your homework and that's it. For two weeks."

"What about the studio?" Finn asked.

"No painting either," his father said. "Got it?"

For a second, Finn looked like he wanted to argue, but then he glanced at Megan and hung his head. "Yeah, I got it."

"All right. Go to your room," John said.

Finn turned and clomped up the stairs. Megan wanted to run after him and thank him, but she didn't think that would look so great.

"John, I'd like to speak to Megan alone, if you don't mind," Regina said, causing Megan to stiffen. She hadn't seen Regina since walking out on her that morning. In all the kissing and chaos, she had nearly forgotten about it.

"Sure," John said. He hesitated a moment and tried to meet Megan's eye, but it took some effort. "I'm not really sure how to put this, so I'm just gonna say it. I'm sorry for my boys' behavior. If anyone ever makes you feel uncomfortable—"

"Oh my gosh, no. I'm fine," Megan said. The last thing she wanted was for John and Regina to think that Finn had somehow taken advantage of her.

"You sure?" John said. "Because I have no problem cracking some skulls if I need to."

"John, she's fine," Regina said with a laugh, putting her hands on his back. "Go watch the game."

"Right. Okay," John said. Then he smiled sheepishly and was gone.

"Don't mind him. It's a testosterone thing," Regina said. "But I guess you're getting a crash course in that."

"Yeah, I guess," Megan said. "Anyway, I'm really sorry about this morning, Regina." Her shoulders finally collapsed as she leaned forward. "I shouldn't have walked out on you like that. It was rude and disrespectful and I'm really sorry."

"You don't have to apologize, Megan," Regina said, sinking into the chair across from hers. "I never asked you if you were interested in the spa before I made the appointments and I should have. So *I'm* sorry."

"You were just trying to be nice," Megan said, a lump of guilt forming in her chest. She knew her parents would be sorely disappointed if they knew how she had treated Regina that morning. "I guess primping and relaxing and all that isn't really my thing," she added, trying to explain.

"And I should have realized that," Regina said, her eyes soft. "I think I was just so excited to have another girl around here—"

"And you got another boy instead," Megan said quietly, staring down at the table.

"No! That's not true," Regina said. She reached out and pulled Megan's hand toward her across the table, forcing Megan to look her in the eye. Regina cupped her fingers over Megan's and held them there. "I got a girl who knows who she is and is really good at being that person."

Slowly Megan smiled, speechless.

"Well," Regina said finally, releasing Megan and standing up. "In this house when someone achieves something like captain of the soccer team, they get to pick dessert."

"How did you know?" Megan asked.

"I bumped into Pearl Porcaro and her mom in the supermarket right after your practice," Regina said with a smile. "So what'll it be?"

Megan thought of her mother. She wasn't a prolific cook, but there were a few things she made incredibly well, and there was one thing Megan loved more than anything else.

"I would kill for some apple pie," Megan said.

"Done," Regina replied.

"I think I'll go call my parents and tell them, if that's okay," Megan said, standing.

"Go ahead," Regina answered. "I'm sure they'll love to hear it."

Megan raced upstairs, bursting with newfound energy. Between the captainship, Finn, the non-grounding, and the Regina moment, she was more than ready to share a little glee. Of course, her parents would only hear about one of the four, but now Megan would sound ten times more excited about it.

As soon as Megan hung up the phone with her parents, there was a knock on her bedroom door.

"It's Finn. Can I come in?" he asked.

Megan's heart started to pound and she slid to the end of her bed. "Yeah. Come in." She smoothed her hair back and wished she had opted for a shower instead of a phone call.

Finn opened the door wide and stood in the doorway.

"Hey."

"Hey."

He was so, so beautiful. Those clear blue-gray eyes, that floppy blond hair. She could still smell him—that mix of freshly washed cotton and tangy paint. Her skin was still warm where his arms and hands had touched her. All she wanted to do was jump him and kiss him again. Was he feeling it too?

"I just wanted to make sure everything was okay," he said.

"Yeah, it's fine," Megan said. "Thank you for . . . what you did down there. You didn't have to."

"Yeah, well. I have some reading to catch up on anyway," Finn said with a small smirk.

Megan looked down at his feet. He was toeing the line between the darker wood floor of the hallway and the light wood floor of her room.

"Do you want to *actually* come in?" she asked.

Finn looked down the hallway to his right. "Um . . . I don't think that's the best idea."

"Oh," Megan said, surprised at the intensity of her disappointment. She understood that he didn't want to get into even more trouble. She did. It was the last thing she wanted as well. Or maybe the second to last. Because right then she would have risked getting grounded for the rest of the year just to be close to him again. Finn clearly wasn't suffering the same way. Otherwise it wouldn't have been so easy for him to resist.

"Well, anyway, I guess I should go back to my cell."

Megan stood up. Maybe if she were closer to him. Maybe then he would remember what it had felt like and he would have to reach out and touch her.

"Okay," she said.

Finn stared into her eyes. *Kiss me,* she thought, trying to force the subliminal message in his direction. *Kiss me, kiss me, kiss me!*

"Hey, Finn! I hope you're not anywhere other than your bedroom!" John called from downstairs.

"Okay," Finn said under his breath. "Well, see ya."

One second he was there, and then a second later the door to her bedroom slammed and he was gone.

On Monday morning Megan walked into the school bathroom and saw the last thing she wanted to see first thing in the morning—Hailey. It was clear from her blotchy face that Hailey had been crying. Now she was leaning over the sink, trying to fix her eyeliner in the mirror. Megan stood there for a moment too long, suspended between the urge to flee and not have this conversation and her newfound compulsion to be tough. But before Megan could decide anything, Hailey looked up. She cleared her throat and said, "Hey."

Megan stepped tentatively into the room. "You okay?" she asked, mostly as a reflex.

"You don't have to act like you care," Hailey said, dropping her eyeliner back into her little mesh bag. She didn't sound sarcastic or belligerent, just tired and sad.

"I'm not acting . . . I don't think," Megan said, leaning back against the sink.

"Well, everyone hates me. It's official," Hailey said with a shrug. She shook her head as she repacked her backpack in a flurry, sweeping a hairbrush and a bottle of spray from the counter. "Even Jessica wouldn't talk to me this morning. She's such a hypocrite. It's not like she didn't know what was going on."

Hailey met her eye in the mirror and pulled her backpack onto her shoulders. She took a deep breath and turned around.

"Look, I'm not going to even try to explain everything to

you," she said, looking more fragile than Megan had ever imagined possible. "It's just, I really love him and I really couldn't imagine what it would be like if he . . . if he . . ."

"It's okay. I get it," Megan said. Except she wasn't entirely sure that she did. After all, she had never been in love herself. Not in a real, requited, relationship love, at least. But the last thing she wanted to do was stand there and watch Hailey totally break down.

"No, you don't. I'm really not like this," Hailey said. "I'm never this much of a head case. It's just . . . it all made sense at the time, you know? It all made perfect sense. But now everything's just all screwed up."

"Well, everybody makes mistakes, I guess," Megan said. She turned and yanked a paper towel out of the dispenser and handed it over to Hailey.

Hailey took it and dabbed a corner under one eye. "Why are you being so nice?" she asked.

Megan blinked. "Honestly, I have no idea."

And then suddenly a strange thing happened—they both laughed. It was a liberating moment for Megan, standing there laughing with her sworn enemy while the girl tried not to cry. Megan just wanted everything to be simple again. There was just no reason for everyone to be so miserable. Plus, after everything that had happened with Finn, Hailey could have Evan and all their drama. Megan was done.

"Well, I'm sorry. About all of it," Hailey said, mashing the towel into a ball. "You have no idea how sorry," she added bitterly, and Megan knew she was thinking about Evan.

Watching Hailey gather her strength, Megan's heart expanded to capacity. She had a feeling that the next few weeks were going to be even worse for Hailey than the last couple had been for Megan.

"Okay," Megan said with a nod. "Thanks."

Hailey let out a breath and launched the paper towel at the garbage can. It swished right in.

"Don't tell me you play basketball, too," Megan said lightly.

Hailey looked at Megan and sighed. "This is going to be one long year."

Megan placed her lunch tray down on the table and looked over at the courtyard. Miller was sitting at his old table with his headphones on, his eyes narrowed in concentration. Megan had been surprised when he hadn't met her by the door like he had all last week, but now she was even more confused. It was like all their progress had been forgotten.

"What's up with Miller?" Ria asked, lifting her messenger bag over her head as she sat down.

"I was just wondering the same thing," Megan said.

"Actually, he said something about not being allowed to sit with you," Aimee said, shaking her apple juice as she looked up at Megan. "What's that about?"

"Not being *allowed* to sit with me?" Megan asked, confused. "That's weird. I'm gonna go talk to him."

"Tell him we miss him!" Pearl said as she popped open her box of beads.

Megan was about to head outside when Hailey appeared, tray in hands, at the end of their table.

"Hi," she said with an overly bright smile.

"Uh . . . hi," Megan replied.

"What's up?" Aimee asked, her brow creased.

"Jessica and those guys are acting all menstrual, so I was wondering if I could sit with you for a few days," Hailey said.

Everyone at the table looked at Megan and she hesitated. Random apologies in the bathroom she could handle. Sitting with the girl at lunch all week seemed like a bit too much to ask. But one glimpse of the almost desperate hope in Hailey's eyes and Megan felt her resolve crumbling. One could only imagine how mortifying it would be for a girl like Hailey to be seen sitting alone in the cafeteria. It was probably her worst fear.

"Sure, I guess," Megan said finally.

Aimee let out a breath. For a few moments, no one spoke. Megan twirled her fork in her spaghetti. The table was so silent it sounded like no one was breathing. Someone was going to have to say something soon or they were all going to suffocate.

"So, everybody ready for our first game?" Aimee said finally.

"You know it," Ria put in.

"They've got a new goalie this year," Hailey said. "She's green, but she's good."

"Coach said she's a lefty, so she's weak to her right side," Megan put in. "We have to go that way as much as possible."

"It must be nice when you guys know their weaknesses," Jenna said, her eyes gleaming behind her glasses.

"Hey, Hailey, want a bracelet?" Pearl asked.

Everyone turned to look at her. Stilted conversation was one thing. Gifts were quite another.

"Uh . . . sure," Hailey said.

She turned and unzipped the small pouch on her backpack. As she dug through it, Ria whacked Pearl on the arm.

"You're gonna make her jewelry?" Ria whispered.

"Ow! What's the big deal?" Pearl whispered back.

"That girl does not deserve presents," Ria replied.

"Well, I can't take it back now," Pearl said, looking miserable.

Megan watched Hailey as her search intensified. There was no doubt she was listening to every hushed word that was being said.

"You know what, you guys? It's okay. I don't need any more jewelry," Hailey declared, whipping out a tube of lip gloss. Something fell out of her backpack with it and landed directly in the center of the table, facing Megan. It was a little patch with burgundy letters and gold piping. It read *CAPT*.

Everyone at the table turned to stone. Megan couldn't have torn her eyes away if she tried.

"What's that?" she said finally.

"Oh, it's just—my mom had it made for me before—you know," Hailey stammered as she picked it up. "It's for my varsity jacket."

She paused and Aimee shifted uncomfortably in her seat. Megan felt like disappearing.

"Whatever, I guess you can have it now," Hailey said, dropping it on the table in front of Megan's tray.

Megan didn't even want to touch it. She thought of her team

back in Texas and how devastated she had been when she realized she was never going to be their captain. She could only imagine what it would have felt like for her to actually have to hand over her captain's badge to someone else. It would have torn her heart out.

"So, did you guys hear that Mr. McKenna is dating Marcy Sherman?" Ria said out of nowhere.

"Ew! Gross!" Pearl exclaimed.

"Who's Marcy Sherman?" Megan asked, glancing at Hailey, who looked up from the captain's patch.

"She used to go here," Hailey said, picking up her water bottle. "She's only two years older than me."

"Ugh! That's just so wrong," Jenna said. "Mr. McKenna is ancient."

The conversation continued to swirl around them and the patch just sat there on the table, seeming to grow larger with every passing second. Megan waited for Hailey to take it back, but she knew that if the roles were reversed, she wouldn't want that thing hanging around in her bag, reminding her of the captainship she had always wanted and almost had. She hadn't forgiven Hailey for everything she had done, but still, her heart went out to the girl. She couldn't believe it was possible to be so angry at someone and feel so badly for them at the same time.

Why did life have to be so complicated?

From: TooDamn-Funky@yahoo.com
To: Kicker5525@yahoo.com
Re: OMG OMG OMG

you kissed FINN??? not evan . . . FINN??? WHEN? WHY? FOR HOW LONG? HOW CAN YOU E-MAIL ME WITH THIS NEWS AND NOT ELABORATE AT ALL? And forget me, where the hell are YOU!!???

----Original Message----
From: Kicker5525@yahoo.com
To: TooDamn-Funky@rockin.com
Subject: OMG OMG OMG

I KISSED FINN! I KISSED FINN! OMG I KISSED FINN. WHERE ARE YOU!!!???

Seventeen

"You sure about this, Meade?" Coach Leonard asked.

"Yeah, Coach. I know it sounds crazy, but I'm doing the right thing."

There was a quick knock on the office door before it opened. Megan turned around as Hailey stuck her head inside.

"Hey, Coach. Vithya said you wanted to see me?" Hailey said. Then she saw Megan and paused.

"Yeah, Farmer. Have a seat," Coach Leonard said.

Hailey dropped into the chair next to Megan's and carefully placed her jacket and her two bags on the floor. She suddenly looked small and scared, like a kid waiting to get a tetanus shot.

"Okay, Farmer, let me get you up to speed. Meade has just told me that the voting for captain may not have been exactly fair," Coach Leonard said, leaning forward in her chair and resting her thick forearms on the desk.

"What do you mean?" Hailey asked carefully.

"I understand that the two of you tied in the first vote and that some kind of gossip affected the second vote," Coach said, looking directly at Hailey. "Would you say that's about right?"

Megan and Hailey looked at each other. Hailey still looked confused.

"Yeah," Hailey said.

Coach Leonard tapped a pencil on the edge of the desk. "Well, I'm sorry to say this has happened before—factors unrelated to our team affecting the vote, that is," Coach said, leaning back in her chair. "But this is the first time in my twelve years here that a captain has ever asked if she could hand over her title to another player."

"What?" Hailey blurted, sitting forward, then turning to look back at Megan. "Are you kidding me?"

"It doesn't make sense for me to be captain," Megan explained, pushing herself up in her seat. "You've been here longer and you've always been the leader of this team. . . . If I hadn't transferred here, you definitely would have won that vote."

"Do you even hear yourself? Do you realize what you're doing?" Hailey asked.

"Yeah, I do," Megan said.

"I don't get it," Hailey said. "I've been so . . ."

She trailed off and they both looked at Coach Leonard, who appeared to be hanging on their every word.

"So what? You've been so what?" Leonard asked.

"Nothing," Megan replied. "Look, Hailey, I'm not saying I want to be best friends or anything, but I just think you should be captain. Besides, you're a senior and I'm a junior. This is your last chance."

Hailey sat back in her chair, dumbstruck. Megan glanced at Coach Leonard. It seemed about time for the authority figure in the room to chime in.

"Well, as much as I love a little drama in the afternoon, we have a game to play, so I'm going to make an executive decision here," Coach Leonard said, pushing some papers together. "Meade, as honorable as this idea of yours is, we can't completely ignore the team's vote, so I propose a compromise. As of right now, the two of you are co-captains. Think you can handle it?"

Megan looked at Hailey. Working side by side with her to lead the team all season? She wasn't entirely sure they could do it without killing each other.

"Sounds fair," Hailey said tentatively.

"We did tie the first time," Megan added.

"All right, it's settled," Coach said. "Now go get into your uniforms and let's kick a little Black Bear butt."

Megan picked up her stuff and opened the door, Hailey trailing behind her. As they walked to the locker room, Hailey took a few extra steps to catch up with Megan and walk by her side.

"You better be ready for this game, newbie," Hailey said, opening the locker room door for Megan and letting the sounds of adrenaline-hyped conversation spill out. She gave Megan a small smile.

"Watch and learn," Megan shot back with a smirk. "Just watch and learn."

Megan raced into the house, practically bursting with her news. Not only had she scored the final goal, but the whole game had been flawless. They had totally dominated the Bears and everyone was talking about how this could really be the year. Hailey and Megan were going to lead them to States. Maybe it was a little premature, but that didn't do anything to squelch Megan's excitement.

A loud, communal groan went up in the basement and Megan barreled down the stairs, breathless. Caleb and Ian had the controls and Caleb was sitting in Evan's lap. Doug was slouched into the couch on the far wall with Miller at the other end, staring down at *Sporting News*. Megan was disappointed to see that Finn wasn't there, but it only tripped her up for a second.

"You guys are never going to believe this! We just beat Hacketstown four to nothing!" Megan exclaimed. "You should have seen it! We were on fire! You guys totally have to come to one of my games. I swear it's gonna be history in the making."

No one said a word. No one even looked at her.

"Hello? Anybody hear me?" Megan said, waving her hand.

Miller's head bent closer to the page. Evan clenched his jaw and stared at the TV screen. Caleb started to squirm as he looked at each of his brothers in turn.

Megan's stomach turned. They were actively ignoring her. And they had somehow gotten Miller in on it. That was why he hadn't been *allowed* to sit with her at lunch that day. Apparently another meeting had been held and the freeze-out was on.

Megan shook her head and looked at the floor. "I don't believe you guys," she said. "What did I do this time?"

"You got Finn grounded," Ian said finally.

"Yeah, and he was gonna teach me how to get past the second level on Halo 2," Caleb groused.

Megan laughed. "You have to be kidding me."

Still, no one would look at her. No one was laughing.

Suddenly Megan felt a rush of something hot and bilious. Her giddiness was washed away by a wave of anger so fierce it completely took over.

"Are you guys going to blame me for everything that happens in this house from here on out?" she asked.

"Finn couldn't covet your cookies if you weren't here shovin' 'em in his face, could he?" Doug said.

"Omigod! Is that what you think happened?" Megan asked. "I seduced him or something? Well, here's a little news flash, Gangsta Boy, *he* kissed *me*, all right? God! Can't any of you take any responsibility for your actions? All I've tried to do since I walked through that door is be your friend, but you're so damn cliquey you've done everything you possibly can to make me miserable. Well, I'm sick of it!"

"Uh-oh, watch out. The little girl's gonna throw a tantrum," Doug said, holding up his hands.

Caleb and Ian laughed and Megan narrowed her eyes at Doug until he had to look away.

"You two don't get to laugh at me," Megan said, walking over to Ian and Caleb. "Do you know how many things you've done since I've been here that I totally could have ratted on you for? You've been in my room, you've trashed my clothes, you've stolen my makeup, you flattened my tires. And who knows what else? But I haven't said a word. I've totally protected your butts."

The boys looked down at the carpet and Megan moved on. "And you, Miller. You wouldn't even be talking to Aimee if it wasn't for me."

"You talkin' to girls now, dill hole?" Doug said.

"And you!" Megan said, whirling on Doug. "Somewhere in that impossibly thick head of yours you know that you owe me big time."

"What the hell is that supposed to mean?" Evan snapped, speaking for the first time.

"Don't even get me started on you," Megan said, her eyes flashing. "I am not the one who slept with your girlfriend, all right? So stop taking it out on me!"

Evan stared at her for a long moment before finally giving up and looking back at the TV.

"God, you guys are so oblivious." Megan shook her head. "All you care about is yourselves. You're not mad at me because I got Finn grounded. You're just looking for another excuse to feel all manly by ostracizing me. Well, let me tell you something, *boys*, you don't look like men to me. You look like a bunch of whiny little babies."

Doug's eyes flashed and when he saw that Megan realized she had gotten to him, he snorted a laugh.

"Oh, great argument, Doug. Very piercing," Megan said, holding her hand over her heart. "You just got me right here."

Leaving them in silence, Megan stomped up to the first floor and all the way up to her bedroom, slamming the door behind her.

I can't believe I just did that, she thought, her mind whirling.

On shaky legs, Megan walked to her bed and collapsed forward. In her mind she saw Evan's angry profile, Doug's sneer, Miller trying as hard as he could not to look at her, Ian staring pointedly at the television, Caleb scowling as he yelled at her. Her relief was tinged by an overwhelming sadness. They had shown her how they really felt. And no matter what she had done, no matter how hard she had tried, they all hated her. They all really, truly hated her.

"It doesn't matter," Megan said aloud. "They're a bunch of jerks." And what did she care if a bunch of jerks hated her? She didn't. She didn't care at all.

Slowly Megan pulled a pillow toward her and pressed her face into it. She spent the next half hour trying as hard as she could not to cry.

Megan slammed her chemistry textbook shut and looked at the clock. In the last hour she had absorbed exactly nothing. Between obsessing about the fact that Finn was right next door and replaying her meltdown that afternoon over and over in her head, there was no room left in her brain for the periodic table of elements.

Dinner had been a silent, tense affair during which Megan had pushed around her chicken and vegetables and sipped at her water. Somehow, eating in the presence of half a dozen people who hated her was just not possible. Now, of course, she was starving.

Megan grabbed her backpack and dug through it until she found the Snickers bar she had bought that afternoon after lunch. She polished it off in four bites, but her stomach was still twisted in knots: it was time to talk to Finn.

He had to have heard about what had happened that afternoon. These brothers were more gossipy than the entire female population of Baker High. She was actually kind of surprised he hadn't already come to talk to her about it, but if he wasn't going to come to her, she could go to him.

She headed out into the hall and knocked quietly on his door.

"Come in!"

Megan took a deep breath and stepped inside. "Hey."

Finn looked up from his desk as if startled. "Hi," he replied, pushing his hands against the thighs of his jeans. He glanced past her at the hallway, but when Megan turned around, she found they were alone.

"What's up?" Megan asked.

"You really shouldn't be in here," Finn said.

Megan's heart dropped like a stone. "I know your parents are mad, but do you think they really expect us not to talk?"

"Yeah . . . no . . . I don't know," Finn said, turning in his chair. "I just . . . Don't you think we should let things calm down a little first?"

"Yeah, like that's ever going to happen in this house," Megan joked lamely. Finn didn't laugh. She swallowed against a lump in her throat and looked around uncertainly. She had come in here so that Finn could reassure her and make her feel better like he always did, but the evasive way he was acting was just making her feel worse.

"Look, it's just . . . being around you is . . . it's not easy," Finn said, looking everywhere but at her. He might as well have thrown cold water in her face.

"Oh, well, I'm sorry," Megan replied, backing out. "I guess that's easily solved."

"No, Megan, wait," Finn said.

But she was dangerously close to tears and there was no way she was going to break down in front of him. "No, seriously, I'll go," Megan said.

Finn swallowed and looked like he wanted to say something. For a split second, Megan's heart dared to hope, but then he turned away and looked down at his notes again.

"Yeah . . . okay," he said.

Finn focused pointedly on his work. This was really happening. Finn really didn't want to have anything to do with her. Finally, feeling like the biggest idiot on earth, Megan made herself move. Amazingly, she made it back to her room without shedding a tear. She closed the door and grasped the handle just to have something to hold on to. It felt like everything was falling away. Everything she cared about, everything she'd thought she knew. Finn was supposed to be her friend. More than that. He had kissed her. He had held her. She had felt so safe around him. He'd been the only person who had never let her down. Now she just felt abandoned—completely and totally alone.

Megan grabbed her phone off her desk and dialed quickly, the trembling of her fingers making it a difficult task. She hit send and brought the phone to her ear, squeezing her eyes shut as tightly as she could. This had to be done before she changed her mind.

"Major Meade here."

The second she heard his voice, she knew she was doing the right thing. She knew where she was supposed to be.

"Dad?" Megan said quickly. "I want to come to Korea. I want to come home."

From: Kicker5525@yahoo.com
To: TooDamn-Funky@rockin.com
Subject: Boy Guide

Megan Meade's Guide to the McGowan Boys
Entry Twelve

Observation #1: Guys make absolutely no sense.
I thought he liked me, Trace. I really thought he liked me.

Eighteen

"You're leaving?"

It was Tuesday evening and Megan's mother had just called to let her know that they had booked her on a Thursday night flight. And now Megan was sitting in the kitchen with Regina and John, who were looking at her like she had just announced an impending sex change operation.

"I talked to my parents and we all just think it's the right thing," Megan said, her heart pounding. She wanted to say as little as possible. There was no way she was going to sit here and face these people who had been so kind to her and tell them that their sons had driven her away.

"We know it hasn't been easy, Megan, but you haven't even really given yourself time to adjust," Regina said.

"Or us," John added. "If there's anything we can do to make you more comfortable, please, just ask."

"It's not that," Megan said. "You guys have been great, really. It's just . . . I miss my parents."

It was an honest reason. Just one of many others that she wasn't going to mention.

"Of course you do, sweetie," Regina said. "But are you really sure you want to move to Korea? When your father first called us, he said you were so adamant about staying."

Megan swallowed hard, trying not to think about all the things she was going to miss. Games with her new team, lunches with Aimee and the others, the parties, the proms. Her father had told her about the school she would be attending in Korea. It was an all-girl school with uniforms and a strict no-makeup policy. Megan was guessing that late-night dances were frowned upon.

Of course, after everything that had happened the past couple of weeks, maybe that would be safer. Maybe Megan needed a boy-free zone for now.

"I just think I made a mistake," Megan said. "It's a lot, you know? At least if I'm with my parents, I'll be . . . I don't know. . . ."

She couldn't figure out how to put it into words without offending them. What she wanted was that comfort level, that familiarity, that feeling she was safe. Her parents could give that to her.

Regina and John exchanged a long look. "Is there anything we can say to change your mind?" John asked finally.

"Not really," Megan said. "But it's nice that you want to try."

Regina let out a sigh and smiled wanly. "Well, we'll miss you," she said. "And I want you to know that you're welcome back here anytime."

Megan smiled her thanks. Both John and Regina looked upset, but Megan knew that deep down, they had to be relieved. As Doug had pointed out to his brothers during her first week there, they had the place wired tight. All Megan had done was come in and get everything all tangled up and confused. She was sure that on some level, the McGowans were looking forward to regaining some semblance of the order they had once had—as chaotic as that order might have been.

"Listen, do you think we could not tell . . . everyone?" Megan said. "I think it would just make everything harder."

What with the massive victory party they would throw and all, she thought.

"Do you really think that's fair?" John asked.

"They won't mind," Megan said. "Trust me. I'll write them an e-mail or something, I promise."

"Well, okay," John said. "I guess we can respect that."

"Thanks," Megan said, standing. "I think I'm going to go start organizing my things."

Megan headed upstairs, her entire body feeling heavy. She had thought she would be relieved after breaking the news to John and Regina, but she just felt sad.

You're doing the right thing, she told herself.

She closed her bedroom door quietly behind her and looked around at her things. It was time to move on.

Thursday evening, Megan sat on the edge of her bed, her bags all packed and neatly stacked on the mattress behind her, her foot bouncing spastically against the floor. She had been ready to go for an hour, but she still had forty-five minutes before the car picked her up. John had offered to take her to the airport, but Megan had declined. She just wanted to get out of here. Make a clean break. Leave everything behind.

Of course, now that the time was approaching, it was obvious that Megan was never going to get out of the house without everyone knowing it. They were all home, going about their normal lives. Megan struggling out of her room with her bags and her laptop was going to turn some heads.

I'll just deal with it. I'll just deal with whatever happens, Megan thought, pushing herself up. She paced the room, knocking her fist against her palm. She felt like she was stuck in that anxious moment before getting up in front of class to do an oral report—times a hundred. Every second Megan wanted to walk out of the room, find Finn or Evan or Doug or even Miller and tell them exactly what she thought of them. This could, after all, be her last chance. But what would be the point?

Megan glanced out the back window and saw Evan swinging listlessly on the hammock, staring up at the sky with one arm crooked behind his head. From his wistful expression she had a feeling he was thinking about Hailey. Megan suddenly felt like smacking him. Two weeks ago, whenever she saw Evan, she'd seen a kind, deep, gorgeous guy with an amazing soul. Now all she saw was a big baby.

Evan knew the truth now. It was all over the school. He knew that Hailey was the one who had lied. But had he apologized to Megan? No. Had he made up with Doug? No. It was like he just *wanted* to be the big, sorry victim.

Standing there, staring down at him, Megan realized that there *was* a point in talking to Evan. Maybe she could return him to a semblance of the guy she had thought she knew. Maybe she could wake him the heck up.

Suddenly determined, Megan raced downstairs and out to

the backyard. The sun was just starting to go down, muting everything around her.

"I need to talk to you," she said as Evan sat up. She turned toward the house. "Hey, Doug! I found one of your old *Playboy*s! If you want it back, I'm outside!"

Evan shoved his way out of the hammock and started past her. "I'm not talking to him."

"Yes, you are," Megan replied, crossing her arms over her chest. "Don't you think you owe me one conversation?"

Evan could barely look at her. "Yeah, maybe you," he admitted finally. "But not him."

Doug came barreling out the back door. The moment he saw Megan and Evan and no *Playboy*, he turned and started back inside.

"I wanted to tell you both that I'm leaving for Korea," Megan announced. "In about half an hour."

Evan's jaw dropped and Doug froze in his tracks. He turned around slowly and plastered a smile on his face. "Finally," he said.

"Yeah, well, before I go, there's something I want to say to you guys," Megan said.

"Famous last words?" Doug asked sarcastically.

But he sat on the edge of a patio chair, his legs wide, and looked up at her expectantly. Evan didn't move either. Megan took a deep breath. She only had one chance to get this right.

"Ever since I was a little kid, I've wanted a brother or a sister," Megan began, looking back and forth between them. "I always thought it would be so great. I'd have someone to share everything with, someone who would always be there, someone who I'd care about and watch out for, who'd care about and watch out for me. But after watching the way you guys have treated each other the past couple of weeks, I don't know anymore."

Evan looked at the ground and Doug rolled his eyes, but Megan didn't stop.

"To let someone like Hailey Farmer . . . something as stupid as meaningless drunken sex come between you guys . . . it's just insane," Megan said. "The girl lied to both of you. She *played* both of you. You guys are brothers. That's a forever thing. And what kills me . . . what really kills me is that you have no idea how lucky that makes you."

Megan looked up. Doug's expression had changed. He and Evan were now both staring at her with hard eyes, as if they were trying very hard to keep what they were really feeling and thinking inside. For the first time Megan was struck by how similar these two seemingly different guys really were. Same stubbornness, same ignorance, and, apparently, same taste in women.

"The truth is, I feel sorry for you guys. I really do," Megan said. "You're all so busy looking out for number one that you don't realize how much you're hurting the people around you. People that really love you. Or could, if you gave them the chance," Megan finished, looking at Evan. She held his gaze until her face burned with the effort and he finally blinked.

Megan turned to Doug. "So don't think that it was your stellar freeze-out that got me to leave, 'cuz it wasn't," she added. "I just can't stand to be around people who take so much for granted."

Aside from the birds in the trees chirping their good-night songs, the backyard was totally silent. Megan had said her piece, and having been that honest, she felt exhilarated. She felt capable of anything. Now, all of a sudden, she had an overwhelming urge to talk to Finn. She turned and, out of habit, walked over to the shed, not even thinking about the fact that he had been banned from his home-away-from-home. One push opened the door and Megan's entire world came to a screeching stop.

Standing on the easel directly across from her was her own image. Finn's painting of her. Completed to the last eyelash. It took her breath away.

Slowly Megan approached the painting. It was unlike anything else Finn had ever painted. He hadn't painted her profile or her shoulder or her hands or her ear. It was the only painting in the room that was a full, face-forward portrait, and it was amazing how much it looked like her. Only softer somehow. Prettier. More open. Her lips were pulled up on one side in a sort of knowing smile. Her skin practically glowed, and the smattering of freckles across her nose actually looked sweet to her. But it was the eyes that killed her. They swirled with at least five shades of green and had delicate gold flecks painted subtly through them. Was this what she really looked like to Finn? Did he really think she was this . . . beautiful?

Megan reached out and touched the edge of the canvas. The paint was completely dry.

When had he had time to finish this? She remembered suddenly that he had been grounded for the past few days. He must have been sneaking out here all week to work on it. And he had finished it. He had actually finished a painting. Of her.

A horn honked in the driveway. Megan's car was here. Early. Ready to whisk her away.

Just go! she told herself, trying to rally the inner troops. *Get the hell out of here already.*

Megan turned her back on her own eyes and ran inside to get her things. This place was more than she could handle. Too confusing, too overwhelming, too much. It was time to go back to a boy-free world.

"Attention, passengers on flight 233, nonstop service to Los Angeles," the gate worker announced. "We are now boarding passengers in rows fifteen to twenty-five. Fifteen to twenty-five, please have your boarding passes ready."

Megan took a deep breath and looked out across the dozens of people gathering their carry-on bags and wrangling their kids. Beyond the seating area for her gate was the concourse that led to the main lobby of the terminal. Megan had been staring in that direction for an hour, much to her own chagrin, thinking she might see a familiar face. That someone, anyone, might come to say a final good-bye. But apparently life didn't imitate movies. In less than twenty minutes she was going to be in the air. Pretty soon, there would be no turning back.

Pulling her backpack straps onto her shoulders, Megan stood up and headed for the long line that snaked away from the gate.

You don't want to turn back, she told herself, squaring her shoulders. It just seemed so wrong that she hadn't gotten to say good-bye to Finn. He had been her best friend at the McGowan house. Her confidant. Her first kiss. She couldn't believe that she was actually getting on a plane to Korea without talking to him one last time.

"Hey! Megan! Wait up!"

Megan's heart leaped out of her chest as she whirled around. There he was, running toward her through the crowd, shoving people aside to get to her. Never in her life had she been so happy to see . . .

Doug.

"Where the hell do you think you're going, yo?"

He doubled over in front of her, sweat streaming down from his temples as he gasped for breath. Megan checked behind him but didn't see anyone else in his trail.

What the . . . ?

"Are you alone?" she asked.

"I gotta sit," Doug said, wheezing.

He backed up clumsily and fell into the nearest vacant chair. Megan stepped out of line and followed him uncertainly. She looked around the terminal, half expecting to find a hidden camera somewhere. This had to be a joke. *Doug* was chasing her down?

"What are you doing here?" Megan asked, narrowing her eyes. "And how did you get through security?"

"I had ta buy a ticket, you belee d'at?" he said, pulling out a little American Airlines folder. "I can go to Chicago now if I want."

Megan sat on the edge of the chair next to his. "Doug, seriously. I have to get on this plane."

"Hey, you wanna bounce, that's your business," Doug said, shoving the crumpled ticket into the back pocket of his jeans. "But hear me out first."

Megan sighed and leaned back. "Okay. You have five minutes."

"All right, look," Doug said. "After you left, me and Evan,

we talked for the first time since all this crap went down and I can't speak for him, ya know? But me? I realized I been kind of a jerk lately."

"Oh, you realized that, huh?" Megan said.

"Let me finish, woman!" Doug said.

Megan suddenly realized what an effort it was taking for him to talk to her at all, so she pressed her lips together and waited.

"I was just pissed at you from jump 'cuz you snaked my room. But I thought on it and I figured out why you irritate me so much," Doug said.

Megan raised her eyebrows. "Why's that?"

"Well, 'cuz you came in there and you did all this stuff, you know? Like stuff no one else can do," Doug said. For the first time since she'd met him, Doug was looking at her and his guard was down. He wasn't making a sneer or putting on a tough front—he was just there, talking to her. "Like you got Miller talking about stuff that's not baseball. And Ian and Caleb are actually afraid of you. And Sean, like, occasionally comes out of the garage now. And my mom? She's a different person since you been there. She's, y'know, calmer or something."

"Really?"

"It's like just having another female around has chilled her out or something, seriously. She's only whacked me upside the head like once since you got here," Doug said.

Megan couldn't help grinning.

"Plus what you did for me . . ." Doug said. "That was pretty cool too. I still don't know why you did it."

"Soft spot for lost causes?" Megan said with a shrug.

"Well, whatever," Doug said. "Thanks."

"You're welcome," Megan said. It was only one word, but she had a feeling he actually meant it.

"So, look, you can't leave," Doug said, sitting up straight and turning toward her. "If you do, Miller's gonna revert and Caleb and Ian are gonna ride roughshod and Sean'll go back to being Ghost Brother and Finn . . ."

Megan's heart slipped. "Finn what?"

"Finn will be destroyed," Doug said, looking her in the eye. "You got that dude all up in a twist, you know that, right?"

"What does that even mean?" Megan asked.

"All's I know is, he found out you left and he locked himself in the shed and barricaded the door. No one's seen him since," Doug said. "When I bolted, Sean and Evan were trying to boost Caleb up onto the roof so he could look through the skylight and make sure the kid wasn't dead or something."

Megan swallowed hard. "Wow."

For a few minutes Doug and Megan sat in their plastic chairs, watching as the line at the gate grew smaller and smaller. Megan slowly turned everything over in her mind. Was it really possible that she had changed the McGowans' lives like Doug had said? She had thought that her presence had only disrupted things, but now it seemed like in some ways, she had actually made things better.

"We always thought it was cool that my mom only had boys, you know?" Doug said, for once dropping his gangsta accent. "Who knew that we actually *needed* a sister?"

Megan looked down at her hands.

"Oh, man! Are you gonna go all blubbery on my ass?" Doug asked.

Megan laughed. "No."

"So are you comin' back with me or what?"

Megan lifted her head and sighed. "I have a few conditions."

"Shoulda known," Doug said, rolling his eyes.

"First of all, I did not sign up for a truck stop bathroom," Megan said. "You guys need to start cleaning up after yourselves in there. No more blood, no more hair, no more random stains that I don't even want identified."

"All right, all right," Doug said. "That it?"

"Hardly," Megan said. "I want a hands-off rule on all my stuff. *Including* my bike."

"Okay . . ."

"And I want everyone to stop calling me Megan C Cups behind my back."

Doug's jaw went slack as he flushed. "How did you know about that?"

Megan raised her eyebrows.

"All right, fine. Is that all?" Doug said.

"You think you can do these things for me?" Megan asked.

"Well, I may have to put the beatdown on a few people, but yeah. No problem," Doug said casually.

"Don't beat down anybody," Megan said.

"Don't tell me how to do my job," Doug said, cracking his knuckles comically.

"Okay," Megan said, standing. For the first time all day, she felt calm—certain. "I'll come back."

"Thank *God!*" Doug said. "Let's get the hell outta this place."

"Oh, wait! One more thing," Megan said, stopping Doug in his tracks.

His shoulders slumped and he turned around. "What? You want my kidney?"

"I want in on the next ultimate Frisbee game," Megan said.

Doug grinned. "You're playin' skins."

Megan grinned back. "We'll see about that."

Megan leaned back into Sean as she gunned the engine on his Harley, racing up Oak Street. The wind pressed a couple of tears from her eyes as she whooped in total, unadulterated glee. She had almost forgotten how much she loved to ride. It was as if she had just regained a limb she had been missing for the past few weeks.

"All right! Let's take it home!" Sean yelled in her ear.

Megan slowed up and turned the bike into the McGowans' driveway. The ultimate Frisbee game on the front lawn was put on pause as Evan, Finn, Caleb, Ian, and Doug all stopped to watch. Megan climbed off the bike and pulled her helmet off, wiping at her face as she laughed.

"You're a natural," Sean said giving her one of his rare grins.

"Thanks," Megan replied.

"Next weekend we go get your Massachusetts permit," he said. "I'll talk to my buddy Deke down at the junkyard and see if he can find you a bike."

"Really?" Megan didn't know which bowled her over more— the offer or the number of words that had just been strung together.

"Heads up!"

Megan glanced left and snatched the Frisbee out of the air before it had a chance to take her eye out.

"Sorry!"

Evan lifted his hand in an apologetic wave before turning and heading for the porch to swig from a jug of water. It was the first acknowledgment Megan had gotten from him since his very awkward apology on Thursday night. He had come to her room after she and Doug had returned and told her he was sorry. Since then, he had avoided her like the plague.

Megan followed him with her eyes and saw that Aimee and Miller were sitting on the front steps next to the refreshments, watching the game. She launched the Frisbee back toward the other boys and waved at Aimee, who grinned and waved back.

"Miller and Aimee. Together on a weekend," Megan said in awe.

"Yeah, that's just weird," Sean remarked, stepping up next to her.

"Yo! You losers playing or what?" Doug shouted from the center of the yard.

"We're in!" Megan replied, jogging over to them.

"All right. It's you, me, and Finn against Evan, Sean, and the twits," Doug said as Megan reached him.

"We're not twits!" Ian protested from a couple of feet away.

"Yeah, you just keep tellin' yourself that," Doug said.

Megan leaned in to the huddle between Finn and Doug. "Do you guys even realize that you're not really playing ultimate?" Megan asked. "I looked it up online and you're doing it entirely wrong."

"We're doing it McGowan style," Doug replied with a knowing nod.

"What does that mean?" Megan asked.

"It's football with a Frisbee," Finn told her. "And at the end of the game we like to high five a lot and make barking noises. No one knows why or when we started it; we just did."

"Ah," Megan said with a smile. It was nice to be near Finn again. It was nice that he was talking to her like a normal human being. Of course, it didn't stop her from wondering what he was thinking.

"So what's the play?" she asked, hoping to focus.

They huddled closer and her arm brushed Finn's and her pulse skittered ahead. They both looked at the spot where their skin had touched and inched away from each other. Megan held her breath.

"All right, I'm faking to Finn and throwing to Megan," Doug said, oblivious. "Let's see what you can do, *Kicker*."

"Yeah, yeah," Megan said sarcastically.

They all clapped and walked over to the line. The second Doug got the Frisbee, Megan broke right, dodging Sean, and raced toward the driveway with Ian and Caleb hot on her heels. She turned around and saw Doug fake the throw to Finn. Evan jumped to block the Frisbee, but it wasn't there. It was rocketing right toward Megan.

She jumped up and grabbed the disk, but the second she came down, Ian and Caleb grasped onto her legs.

"Get 'em off me!" Megan shouted, struggling forward and laughing uncontrollably. "Get 'em off me!"

"Die, Kicker! Die!" Ian shouted, holding on for dear life.

Finn rushed over and Megan tried to toss the Frisbee to him.

He let it fly right past his face and instead grabbed Caleb, tickling him until he had to let go of Megan.

"Foul! No fair!" Ian shouted.

Caleb rolled on the ground, giggling, and Megan tripped over him and tumbled forward, taking Finn down with her. It was a huge mass of tangled arms and legs, but all Megan knew was that she was right on top of Finn, her chest pressed against his, his leg between her thighs, her wrist pinned under his neck. Someone—Ian—was on her back, holding her down, preventing her from extricating herself.

Not that she exactly wanted to.

"Well, this is awkward," Finn said with a laugh, trying to sit up. "Ian! Get off her!"

"All right!" Ian said, rolling free. Ian snatched the Frisbee from the ground and he and Caleb took off across the yard, holding it high.

Finally Finn was able to sit and Megan rolled away from him, sitting in the dirt at his side. They both fought to catch their breath, though Megan's oxygen deprivation had nothing to do with the game.

"You okay?" Finn asked.

"Yeah, you?" she replied. Every inch of her body was throbbing to touch him again.

"Yeah," he replied with a huge grin. He pushed himself around and got on all fours in front of her, pausing there with his face just inches from hers. "I'm glad you stayed," he whispered his breath warm on her face.

Megan somehow managed to reply. "Me too."

Then Finn pushed himself up and headed back toward the center of the yard. For a moment, Megan couldn't move. Then Doug walked over and offered his arm. Megan grasped it thankfully and he yanked her up to her shaky legs.

"Who's all in a twist now?" he asked with a smirk.

Megan laughed and shoved him from behind as they headed back to the line.

"Dude! I wanna trade!" Doug shouted. "Finn for Sean!"

"You got it," Evan replied.

"Get your head in the game," Doug said to Megan.

Megan shrugged him off and lined up, this time directly across from both Finn and Evan. Finn smiled openly at her and Megan grinned, her heart pounding. But when she looked at Evan, it stopped completely. He was staring at her with those intense eyes. Staring right into her. Just like he had in those couple of moments when she had thought, for a split second, that he wanted to kiss her.

Well, that's . . . interesting, Megan thought.

Doug took the Frisbee. With a deep breath, Megan stood up and dodged right between Finn and Evan, racing upfield. They both took off after her. The Frisbee took flight, sailing in a perfect arc over the boys' heads. All three of them leapt into the air and reached for it, but it was Megan who outran them all and plucked it right out of the sky.

From: Kicker5525@yahoo.com
To: TooDamn-Funky@rockin.com
Subject: Boy Guide

Megan Meade's Guide to the McGowan Boys
Entry Thirteen

Observation #1: Boys are unpredictable.
This may not be news, but I'm starting to think it's one of the
best things about them.